ᴴAINT
BLUE

ꟻAIRY ᴛALES OF A ᴛRAILER ᴘARK ꟴUEEN
ᴮOOK ᴺINE

ᴷIMBRA ꟄWAIN

HAINT BLUE

FAIRY TALES OF A TRAILER PARK QUEEN, BOOK 9

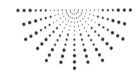

KIMBRA SWAIN

CRIMSON SUN
PRESS

Kimbra Swain
Haint Blue, Fairy Tales of a Trailer Park Queen, Book 9
©2018, Kimbra Swain / Crimson Sun Press, LLC
kimbraswain@gmail.com

Book Cover by: Audrey Logsdon
Editing by Carol Tietsworth: https://www.facebook.com/Editing-by-Carol-Tietsworth-328303247526664/

CHAPTER ONE

LEVI

NOTHING WORSE THAN DRY, RUBBERY SCRAMBLED EGGS WHEN YOU were feeling down. Luther was a great cook, but today, they just didn't taste right. Then again, I figured I was the problem. Nothing was going to taste right. Not today.

"Why the sour face, honey?" Betty asked.

"You know why," I said.

"Well, that's the jist of it, isn't it? Life is precious. Even fairy lives. We are all going to miss Dylan because he meant a lot to each of us in such a short time. Tonight will be difficult," she said.

"Not for me. For her," I said.

"Don't dismiss your own grief, Levi. He was family to you as well. Despite loving the same woman, or perhaps because you both loved her, you and he were thick as thieves. He trusted you with her and his children. I know that weighs heavy on you," she said.

"It does," I said as I pushed the eggs around on the plate.

For me, it was more than just grief. I felt guilty, too. I'd never wanted Dylan dead, especially him not being able to enjoy his son. I supposed it was a heroic death, but I thought he deserved better.

After his story about taking out the old school vamps in Greece, I'd hoped to see him throw down. Even Luther said he was impressive as hell. Now, I was left with all the things he'd told me, especially the wedding dream.

I didn't understand how he could have had the dream without being there himself. After we talked to Mike, we realized the liquid that he had provided to induce the dream was actually a prophetic dream serum. So, Dylan had the dream, seeing what would happen at the wedding. I couldn't accept it as fact. The future wasn't written like that. I had had high hopes, but none of them mattered now. Grace was shattered into pieces, and my only hope was that she would be whole again.

Betty was right though. She wasn't the only one grieving. Many of us here loved Dylan. He was the best of us. His abilities were unheard of, and now that they were split between his children, no one would ever carry a legacy as he had. I couldn't imagine the pressure he was under to produce an heir. Had Winnie not died, he could have made her his heir and carried on with us all.

Which brought to the forefront of my mind, that now, Winnie had those gifts. Well, at least, the Firebird parts. Our sweet little Winnie was now a pistol. Grace hadn't had time to grieve. Aydan was growing by leaps and bounds, and Winnie struggled with controlling her powers. She hadn't burnt anything down, yet. I figured it was only a matter of time.

As I looked down at my plate, another plopped down beside it. The dark hands of Luther Harris came into view. I looked up at his kind eyes. Just by looking at him, you would have never known the power he held inside.

"Sorry. I'm off my game today. Here's a fresh batch," he said.

"No worries. I've not got much of an appetite," I said, but he took the old eggs and slid the new ones in front of me.

"Eat. You look pale," he said.

"No offense, Luther, but nothing tastes right," I said.

"You can't take care of her and the kids if you don't take care of yourself which is why you're here, isn't it?" Luther asked.

"Sort of. I had to get out of the house. We go back and forth between the trailer and the house. She's gone on with being the Queen and a mother despite her pain. I'm afraid tonight will be the breaking point," I said.

"At least she agreed to the memorial," Luther said. "Heavens knows we've had too many for Dylan."

"This one is real," I said.

"Yes, it is, and that's why she is doing it," Luther said.

"She is doing it because Winnie has begged her to do it," I said.

"How's Aydan?" Luther asked.

"Growing. Fast. Too fast."

"Faster than a fairy?"

"Tabitha says yes. He's walking. Still not talking though," I said.

"Grace has her hands full," Luther said.

I took several bites of the new plate of eggs. These were better than the first ones.

"And Winnie?"

"She's still adjusting," I said.

"I think I might be able to help with her. If you would, mention it to Grace. I kinda have experience dealing with fiery beasts," Luther said. I knew that Luther had a handful of his own children. I had wondered if they were all Ifrits like their father.

"I'll tell her. She has been a handful," I said.

"Luther, leave that man alone. He's trying to eat his breakfast," Betty said.

"He's not bothering me. It's nice to talk," I said.

Luther patted me on the back. "Anytime, Son."

He rose from the stool and went behind the counter to cook for others who had arrived. I didn't notice who had come in until Riley sat down next to me.

"Mornin'," she said.

"Hello, Riley," I replied. Not sure why she chose now to speak to me. She had been back from the Otherworld for months.

"How are you?" she asked.

"Fine. How are you?" I replied politely.

"I was really asking, Levi. You look terrible," she said.

"Thanks," I replied.

"I mean it. You look tired," she said.

"I am tired, Riley," I said looking up at her.

Making eye contact with her, my mind was flooded with memories of the two of us together. The sex had been great, but she had used me to get the songbook. It had been more than that for me, so it hurt just sitting here next to her. I didn't want to be rude, but I certainly didn't want to make nice.

She reached up to touch the scar on my face, and I backed away from her.

"Don't," I said. "What do you want?"

"You don't have to be rude," she fussed.

"Riley, I'm tired. I've got a lot on my mind. If there is something I can do for you, please tell me. If not, I ask that you don't touch me. You lost that privilege when you used me to get *that* book."

She stared at me as if I had hurt her deeply. It didn't matter if I had. I wasn't up for playing games today.

"You were never rude, Levi. What has she done to you?" she asked.

"Luther, thanks for breakfast. Catch ya later, Betty," I called out, ignoring Riley's statement.

"Levi, I'd like to make it up to you," Riley said.

I leaned down over her, looking into her emerald green eyes. She shuddered as I moved closer to her. "Riley, you had your chance with me, and you blew it. Don't expect me to make the same mistake twice."

As I walked to the door, I heard her say, "Nothing has changed. She still doesn't want you."

Backing away quickly, I paced out of the diner and climbed on my Harley. Watching Riley through the window, she never turned to look at me. She wasn't wrong, but that wasn't the point. It didn't matter how many Rileys came along. No one but Grace would ever be enough for me. If I had to wait until forever, that was exactly what I was going to do. Even if it meant turning into my father.

CHAPTER TWO

GRACE

BLACK. SUCH A MORBID COLOR. I SUPPOSED THAT'S WHY YOU WORE it to funerals. This wasn't exactly a funeral as much as a memorial. This town had had two other memorials for Dylan. One I went to while the other I avoided. However, this one was real.

Looking at myself in the mirror, I realized Astor was right. I was looking thin. He had commented on it yesterday as he and Ella washed dishes. She had been at the house a lot lately spending time with him. They seemed to be hitting it off quite well, which in the midst of all this sadness, gave me a little light of hope for the future.

My brightest light was my son, Aydan who was growing faster than I ever imagined. He was the happiest little boy on earth. His sister, on the other hand, had turned into quite the handful. She wanted to try out new things, like flying! Something I knew nothing about. Bramble and Briar were eager to help, but soon they found that singed wings were no fun. I wondered how all the other Phoenix children learned to control their powers. It was something that Dylan and I never got a chance to talk about. There were so many things we never had the chance to do. The biggest one was raising our children together.

The low rumble of Levi's Harley approached the house. He'd left this morning in full brood mode, and he'd been gone all day. He was hurting like the rest of us. I regretted making him kill Dylan. In those final moments, all I could think about was hoping for a last-second miracle, but I knew that this time Dylan's death was permanent.

I smoothed the dress out, then put on my teacup necklace. The memorial wasn't until later tonight, but I decided to go ahead and get dressed now. Levi's heavy footsteps came up the stairs but paused at Aydan's room. He was lying down for a nap.

Another few footsteps, then a light tap on the door.

"Come in," I said.

Levi walked in with Aydan who was wide awake.

"Look who I found standing up in the bed," Levi said with a smile.

"I'm surprised he isn't climbing out of it," I said. Aydan smiled and reached for me. When I reached to grab him, Levi pulled him away making him giggle.

"No, you don't want your momma," he teased.

I smiled at the game. Each time Aydan reached for me Levi pulled him away. His sweet laughter filled the room. That was my hope for the future. For days when both of my children could laugh.

"Now, do you want Momma?" Levi asked Aydan who reached for me again. His little hands opened and closed. "You have to say it."

"Levi, he's not going to say it," I said.

"Sure, he will. Aydan, do you want Momma?" he asked.

Aydan opened and closed his mouth, but nothing came out.

"Maybe next time," I said.

"Maybe," Levi said, sounding defeated. He'd been trying to get him to say Momma for days. He just wasn't ready. As much as I wanted to hear him say it, at least it was one thing that seemed to be progressing at a normal speed. My 4-month-old looked like a toddler. Tabitha was pleased with his development despite the fact he wasn't talking.

"What's wrong?" I asked. "Where have you been all day?"

"I went to eat breakfast at the diner, then I just rode around town. When I drove past the Santiago place, Deacon flagged me down to show me that the crops had recovered from the evil eye curse. They should have a good harvest. Then, I stopped to help Mrs. Frist who had a flat tire. She still freaks me out every time I talk to her. Then, I drove around a bit before heading back here. I need to get a shower before the memorial," he said. "I didn't mean to be gone all day."

"I survived," I said.

"I didn't mean it like that," he said.

"I know. Just the same. You don't have to babysit me," I said.

"I like babysitting you," he grinned, but his smile faded quickly.

"I see that. What's wrong?" I asked.

"Riley was in the diner today," he replied.

"She's kept quiet since we got home from Summer," I pondered.

"Yes, well, she wasn't quiet today," he said.

"What did she say?" I asked.

"Nothing that matters," he huffed.

"Levi," I scolded.

"Really, Grace. She's just trying to get under my skin," he said.

"I'm sorry," I replied. Whatever she said to him had to do with me. If I knew Riley, she taunted his loyalty and affection for me. Scorned bitch.

"Don't do that. You haven't done anything wrong," he said.

"I know, but you're hurting like the rest of us. I wish I could take it from you," I said. I reached up to touch his cheek. Pressing my hand against the scar on his face, he leaned into my palm.

"Tonight will help. It will give us all a chance to say goodbye," he said.

"Yes, then we need to get back to business," I said.

"Oh, I did go by and see the prisoner, too. I wanted to see if she was ready to talk," Levi said.

"And?" I asked.

"She wasn't," he replied.

"That's too bad. Because I'm going to make her talk," I said. I saw a flash of worry in Levi's eyes. He knew the darkness inside of me too well. He knew what I was capable of doing. I didn't care that she was my grandfather's girlfriend. Mable Sanders and I were about to have a reckoning.

～

Astor and I waited downstairs as Levi finished his shower. Winnie ran around the room with a ton of energy. She was bouncing off the walls lately, and there was little we could do to calm her down. I was going to have to take her out of school because she wouldn't calm down long enough to learn what she needed. It made things awkward when Ella was around, but she knew we were struggling with what to do with our new little Phoenix child.

"I don't even think I had that much energy at my peak," Astor said.

"Are you saying you aren't at your peak now?" I asked.

"Well, I think my first life was a bit livelier than this one," Astor said.

"That's because you haven't had your way with Miss Ella yet," I said. He blushed brighter than a whore in church.

"You don't know that, Grace," he protested.

"But I do. If there is anything I know, Astor, it's sex, and you aren't having it," I said.

"Well, perhaps I'm just being a gentleman. Waiting until she is ready," he declared.

"Really? That woman has been ready," I said.

"You think so?" he asked.

"Lord have mercy, yes," I replied.

"She looooooooooooves you," Winnie said.

"See, even she notices," I said.

"The Queen's assessment is accurate, Sir Knight," Bramble added as he, Briar, and Rufus chased after Winnie romping around the ground floor of the house.

"Okay, enough," Astor said.

"I've been wondering, Sir Knight, do you plan on picking a last name anytime soon?" I asked.

"Is it necessary?" he asked.

"I suppose not, but if we ever venture out of Shady Grove it helps to have identification with your name on it. Remy can get all the paperwork you need," I said.

"Is Knight a proper last name?" he asked.

"If that's what you want, I suppose it is," I smiled. Astor was simple, but not a simpleton. I loved that about him.

"You all call me Knight anyway," he said.

"Astor Knight," I said.

"You've got to be kidding me," Levi said as he came down the steps.

"Do you not like it, Bard?" Astor asked.

"Seems kinda obvious," Levi said.

"Like Rearden isn't?" Astor said.

I looked at Levi who shrugged. "I didn't name myself," he said.

"It is interesting though. Rearden was your mother's husband's last name, correct?" Astor asked.

"Yeah," he said. His father who was a love talker had an affair with his mother. She hid the fact from him that he was the offspring of a fairy. He grew up with a domineering man who ended up leaving his mother. William, his real father, still lived in Shady Grove drinking away what was left of his life. Unfortunately, it would take a very long time to drink his life away as a fairy. Prolonging the agony for Levi. At one time, I had hoped to talk some sense into him. He seemed to like me better after it, but it didn't change his drinking habits.

"Sorry," I said.

"It's okay," he replied.

"You look nice," I said. I hadn't seen him in a suit since Dylan's first funeral.

"He looks handsome," Winnie said, running up to him. He reached down to pick her up off the ground and she wrapped her arms around his neck. I felt his emotions shift. The strength he'd fortified himself with upstairs was fading with a hug from a child.

"*Hang in there,*" I said.

"*I'm supposed to be telling you that,*" he said.

"*Exactly. So, get your act together,*" I said offering him a half-hearted smile.

"I'm ready to go," Winnie declared. Levi sat her down, and she ran to the door. "Come on, Momma. I can't wait to light all the lanterns."

Astor put on the jacket for his suit which he had borrowed from Tennyson. It was the only one we could find on short notice that would fit him. Tennyson gladly obliged and promised to have a few more made for him.

I gathered Ayden up who looked adorable in his little white shirt and bowtie. Winnie grabbed Levi's hand and dragged him out the door. We followed along to the truck and took the short drive back to the field where it all happened.

CHAPTER THREE

WINNIE, BLESS HER LITTLE HEART, WAS DOING WELL CONTROLLING her fire. It got out of hand sometimes, but when she was focused, she could produce it in a stable environment. The field where Dylan died had filled with the citizens of Shady Grove. Each group of people held a paper lantern with a flaming bird painted on the outside. Winnie loved the cartoon movie with the flying lanterns, and she wanted to have lanterns for Dylan. I couldn't deny her. Not to mention, how perfect I thought the idea was after she mentioned it.

She skipped to each family, couple, or solo member of the community lighting the fires for the lanterns by her own hand using the gifts her father had given her. Watching her, my heart pounded in my chest. So many intensely sad moments since Dylan died had filled our lives, but this one, I couldn't have imagined the ache. As darkness fell, the only lights in the field were Dylan's lights.

Each lantern represented a life he had touched. His warm and giving spirit spread to the entire town. I didn't know of anyone who didn't love him. What was left of him now lived on in our children. It was a heavy burden if I thought about it for too long. My responsibility, not only to raise two children, but to raise them without their father in a way that would make him proud. Then there was all the "Queen" stuff. He believed I could do it, and I had to honor his faith in me by giving it my best shot.

Tears streamed down my face, and I didn't dare hold back. It was time to mourn. Time to remember. Tomorrow, it would be time to fight. I had a fire, too. More than ever before. It was time to take back what was rightfully mine from those who sought to destroy me and my family. No more victims. If someone fell in battle, at least we would be going down fighting. I had a few schemes of my own. Thankfully, I'd made friends with a few schemers. It was time.

Levi stood close by, but not close enough for me to touch. Nestor stood next to me, so I leaned on him. He hugged me close to the side of his body as Winnie finally came up to light our lantern.

"Please don't stay behind me," I begged Levi.

"I didn't want to intrude," he said.

"If we weren't standing in the middle of a funeral, I'd jerk a wart on you," I said.

"Better than jerking a knot in my tail," he smirked as he moved closer.

Nestor and I held the lantern with Levi joining to my side. Winnie lit the lantern, and I felt the tug as it naturally pulled toward the sky. I held it back as if holding it for another moment, would hold Dylan here for another moment.

"Let it go, Momma," Winnie said. Aydan wiggled in my arms reaching for the flickering light.

She had instructed everyone to wait until she let her lantern go. She wanted hers to be first. So, reluctantly, I lifted my arm to the sky as the lantern took flight. Aydan's chubby arms stretched skyward for the light as it moved upward.

Suddenly, the sky was filled with the silent lanterns lifting towards the Heavens. Our tribute to Dylan floated upward to show the world around us that someone important had passed through our lives. He had changed my life completely. Instead of running from place to place, I'd found a home and a family. A purpose.

Nestor tugged tighter as my lip trembled. Aydan patted my face as if he knew Momma was hurting. Levi stood in my shadow ready to catch me if I fell. My knees wobbled, but I shook my head refusing to give in.

Kadence Rayburn led her now blind father to the center of the circle. A dark cloth covered where his eyes used to be. Kady blamed herself for the damage and had moved back in with him. Caleb had as well to help them both. I was impressed with his generous spirit. Matthew assured his daughter that everything that happened to him was his own fault. However, I silently took the blame too. I felt like I could have done more. Should have done more.

Matthew's Druid voice filled the field as if we were in his church.

"Kady tells me that the lights lifting to the sky are beautiful. I wish I could see them, but I know that it is a fitting tribute to our friend, Dylan Riggs. He was a light and a fire for all of us in this town. He came here with his own agenda, but soon made friends and fell in love. His family standing before us is a tribute to the legacy that he lived and leaves behind. Grace, Winnie, and Aydan, you're a part of us just as he was. We give you our deepest sympathies and open our hearts to you. Whatever you have need of, please ask. We are here for you. If it weren't for you, Dylan would have never called Shady Grove home. We are proud that he was one of us until the very end. May the four corners bless you and keep you," he said.

"Bless you and keep you," many members of the town repeated.

Matthew had asked me if I wanted to speak, and I told him that this was to be about him. Not about me. He waited for a moment to see if I had changed my mind, but I remained silent except for the sniffles. Kadence then, led him over to where we stood. He shook Nestor and Levi's hands, then kissed the back of mine. Winnie hugged him around his legs.

"If you need anything, Grace, I'm willing to listen. It seems my ears work quite well," he said with a smile. He had told me when we talked about the memorial that he had found a new hope in his blindness. I couldn't understand it, but he seemed to be at peace. I offered to turn him, but he refused. He believed he was living his destiny, no matter how cruel it had turned out to be.

One by one the members of the community came to offer condolences. Occasionally, I'd look to the sky to keep an eye on the lanterns as they faded into the distance. Switching to my sight, each fire flamed with supernatural light.

"*Look at them through your sight,*" I said to Levi.

"*I see them. They are magnificent,*" he said. I could feel his sorrow. Sometimes I thought perhaps it was worse than my own. He knew all the logical reasons why things turned out the way they did, but he still searched his thoughts trying to find an alternate solution. Bless it. I didn't understand why other than he wanted me to be happy again. I wanted the same for him, but I knew that meant that I would have to find some joy in our lives. Other than my children, it was hard.

Somewhere in my heart, I knew that my life would continue, but it would be a long time before I was truly happy. Right now, I was just hanging on.

CHAPTER FOUR

WHEN WE RETURNED HOME, YOU WOULD HAVE THOUGHT THE Baptist Church was having dinner on the grounds. The kitchen and dining room were covered up with homemade dishes. The house filled with some of our closest friends who picked through the food, but mostly stood around talking about Dylan. Nestor sat on the couch with Aydan playing with toys while Winnie, Mark, and some of the other kids from school played outside with Bramble and Briar. Rufus had decided to hide upstairs. Deacon had appointed himself the outside guard and stood watching the children play in his dirty overalls.

Astor stood in the corner of the dining room with Ella, Mayor Jenkins, and Chaz. The lion hung on his knight as if he were a coat on a hanger. That train of thought led me in the wrong direction, so I focused back on the group. They seemed to be getting along very well. I was happy to see it. I had worried so much about Astor and his finding a purpose. He'd been giving me great advice along with the rest of my war council as we started to make plans to take back Winter from Brockton, my Uncle.

"Do you need anything?" Amanda asked.

"No, everyone has been great. We will never eat all of this

food," I said. "You're welcome to take some of it to the wolves. How many are there now?"

Amanda kept me informed of the shifters as they moved into town. The wolf population had grown exponentially. We still had a few bears, the Purcells, and a unique were-possum. However, Levi, my secretary, hadn't informed me of any new arrivals lately. Levi read all my emails because he knew I never did. He elbowed me as we stood talking to Amanda and Mark.

"There are 28 in all now. Plus, the Santiagos, and the Purcells. Kwaski hasn't been able to get in contact with any of his kin, so he's still our only possum. We've had a family of panthers move in this past week. Is there a point where you don't want anyone here?" she asked.

"No, I don't want to shut anyone out. I suppose at some point we might run out of land, but not anytime soon," I said.

"We aren't worried about space. I'm only concerned about policing them," Troy said. "I have a handle on the wolves. If we start getting an influx of beings that aren't our kind, I'm not sure my alpha status will hold them."

"We will be cautious with everyone, but welcoming. That's the way we do things," I said. "It leaves the door open for Brock to make a move in that department, but I don't want to shut anyone out."

"I'm watching the new comers too closely. He won't get in that way," Amanda said confidently.

"Thank you, Amanda," I said.

"Just doing my job, ma'am," she said with a smile. It wasn't so long ago that she wouldn't have smiled at me. Her skills for organization were invaluable, and our children were BFFs. We needed to get along. I'm glad that we finally did.

They moved away from me, as I felt Levi step closer.

"*You are the strongest woman I've ever known,*" he said.

"*You haven't known many women,*" I replied.

"*I watched my mother battle cancer with dignity, Grace. Don't knock the compliment,*" he said.

Turning to face him, his dark eyes met mine.

"I'm sorry," I muttered.

"Don't be. You're just being you," he dismissed it.

Before we could say anything else, Jenny walked up, but Tennyson remained across the room with his eyes on us. Since reconnecting with him, Jenny had updated her wardrobe. She looked like a mob boss' wife. High dollar dress and shoes and she pulled it off perfectly.

"You have plenty of people here if you need anything. We are going to slip out," she said.

"Sure. You're right. I'm almost ready for some quiet," I said.

She hugged me tightly. "Whatever you need, just call. You know that we have your back," she said. I had told her about my experience with Wendy and the crystal ball. She said the conversation I had seen was real and exact. It was nice to know that there were at least a few people I could absolutely count on. Tennyson's connections in the Otherworld were providing us with the right kind of information for a takeover. Unfortunately, none of the news was good. It was going to take a huge effort, and I wasn't sure how many in town were willing to join the fight.

"Thanks, Jenny," I said. She backed away, winked at Levi, then rejoined Tennyson. He gave me a nod across the room, and they slipped out.

"Grace, have a drink," Betty said, handing me a glass. It was short with just a couple of cubes of ice and a dark liquid. Perfect. I took a sip, allowing the burn to race down my throat.

"When should I expect Winnie?" Luther asked.

"Huh?" I said.

"I forgot to tell her," Levi said.

"Oh, I would like to offer my help with Winnie. We are fire beings. She will respond to me, if you will allow it," Luther explained.

"Luther, I can't ask you to step in like that," I said.

"Grace, we are family, remember? I want to help. Besides, I'm not doing it for you. I'm doing it for Dylan," he smiled. The devil knew I couldn't deny him now.

"Very well. When would you like to start?" I asked.

"As soon as possible before she burns the house down," he said.

"Yes, please," I replied.

"We can set it up later. Just let us know," Betty said.

"Sure," I replied, as Aydan giggled at Nestor across the room. I watched them playing. Aydan was having a grand time with all the attention. I could feel Winnie outside playing with the children. Her warmth now reminded me every moment of Dylan. My children were my life now. Everything I did from this moment on was about them. My own desires, hopes, and dreams had long faded but were now replaced with hopes and dreams for them. Even though Winnie struggled with her new abilities, I knew one day she would be the same shining beacon her father was. And even though, in less than 5 years, Aydan would be a full-grown adult, I was going to cherish every moment between now and then.

And I was going to the Otherworld not just to take my inheritance, but, as Cletus would say, open a fat can of whoop ass. One of those bulk-sized cans.

"Grace?" Betty said.

"I'm sorry. I zoned out. What did you say?" I asked.

"Get some rest, honey. If you need anything, we are close by," she said with a smile, then tugged Luther away.

I turned away from the crowd heading toward the back door. When I stepped out on the porch the air was cool. The children were running around the yard chasing fireflies, and for once, Winnie wasn't the flying fire. They were actually chasing bugs. I watched their simple game until a mosquito bit the tar out of my arm.

I smacked my hand down on my arm smashing the bastard. "Serves you right," I hissed.

"Y'all come inside. It's swarming skeeters out here," I called out to the kids. They came running like a herd of pigs. Whooping and hollering. Laughing and playing. I held the door for them as they all went inside. Looking in at all of my friends and family, my heart was warmed, but a coldness sealed my mind. Instead of going back inside, I pulled power from my tattoo to shield myself from the tiny flying vampires and made my way to the swing set.

The wonderous sounds of people fellowshipping in my home

drifted out of the walls. I sat down in a swing watching the warm lights in the house, and the shadows of the people passing the windows. With a small movement of power, I saw my bard appear on the back porch.

"*Let's talk about it,*" I said. We hadn't talked about Dylan's revelation about the wedding dream. It bothered Levi. I could only assume that he knew what Dylan had dreamed because Dylan told him. I didn't want it hanging over us. Not to say it didn't bother me, it just made things very awkward between us. I couldn't ignore the feelings I had for Levi, but more than anything, my heart was secondary now. It was in too many pieces to be what he needed.

"*It's not necessary. Don't stay out here too long,*" he said.

"*Levi, I want to. Maybe I need to,*" I said.

Instead of skipping over to me, he stuck his hands deep into his pockets and trudged over to me like he was walking through mud. He'd shed the tie and jacket from earlier. The man before me wasn't the same as when he came to Shady Grove. He wasn't the same man that went into the Otherworld and fought Dylan in his hysteria. He wasn't the same man since Dylan died on that field.

He took a seat on the swing next to me, and for a few moments, we sat in silence watching the fireflies. I saw Finley peek out one of the curtains. I waved at him, and he ducked back inside. Hopefully, he took that as "leave us the hell alone." Which is what I meant.

"He told you," I said.

"He did," Levi said. "The future isn't written though. How many times did he dream that the two of you would get married before he lied about it?"

"I'm not sure," I said. "What he dreamed doesn't concern me as much as the impact that it has on us."

"You told your father that we were solid," he said.

"We are. Dylan's dream doesn't change that," I said.

We rocked back and forth on the swings. The katydids filled the air with their song, along with the low croaking of frogs. The night songs of the Southern countryside. It made me sad knowing that my goal to take back the Otherworld would more than likely take me away from this. Shady Grove was home, and it always would be.

The silence wore too long for Levi and his anxiety kicked up. "Grace, I don't assume anything. You know how I feel about you, but I'm not an idiot. He died. I killed him. In fact, I should have done it down in the Otherworld as he asked me to do, but I wasn't man enough to do it then. Coming home to you was my only consolation after all of that. You have a kingdom to take and one to rule. I'm not an idiot."

"Yes, you are," I said. "Dublin. Yes, you are."

"Damn you, Grace," he huffed standing up to leave me alone, but he stopped in his tracks dropping his shoulders and head to the ground.

I eased up out of the swing, walking around to face him. If my heart wasn't in a billion pieces, I'd reassure him like he deserved to be reassured.

Placing my hand on his scarred cheek, I turned his eyes to mine.

"Dylan died. You did not kill him. He died to save my daughter, and you helped him do it. I will be forever grateful for that. I need you, Dublin. Whatever dream he had doesn't matter, because there is a big fat war coming, and whether we admit it or not, we might not survive it. But if I go down fighting, I want you with me. We can die together. It will be all epically romantic and shit," I said.

He huffed again, shaking his head at me. "You know how to motivate a guy," he said.

"Actually, I do, but we won't go there," I said. "I'm not worried about some stupid wedding dream."

Letting out the longest brooding sigh I'd ever heard, he lifted his eyes to the stars and said, "It wasn't a dream though. It was a prophecy."

"Huh?" I immediately countered.

Before he could explain, a cool breeze surrounded us like a dark cloud. The strings on his guitar tattoo came to life forming a barrier around us. We turned around looking at the gathering darkness.

"What the fuck," he muttered. "I feel them."

"What is it?" I asked, allowing power to build up in my tattoo. I felt panicked movements in the house. "*Astor! Protect my children!*"

"*I have them, my Queen,*" he quickly answered.

The back door started to rattle. I could feel Finley yanking on it trying to open it. Opening my sight, I could see forms slinking across the ground toward us. Their eyes glowed bright white. Their bodies undulated from beneath the surface of the ground to the grass but were nothing but shadows of men. Not actual men.

Levi's back pressed into mine. "They are all around us, but I can't skip," he said. "My home spell won't work because we are already home."

"Just stay calm. They haven't attacked," I said.

A column of black smoke rose in front of me just outside Levi's barrier, coalescing into a form more like a man. His white eyes focused on me.

"Queen of this realm. You have some that belong to us. We have come to collect. You have until the full moon to release our prize to us, or we will come after it," it said.

"I don't know who the fuck you are, but get out of my town," I said.

"*Perhaps a little more diplomatic,*" Levi suggested.

"Please," I added which caused Levi to snort.

"Your brashness is noted. We will come for you all if we don't get our due," it said.

"Bring it, smoke boy," I said.

Its shoulders shook as if it had laughed at my challenge. I wasn't trying to be funny, but whatever works.

"Be gone!" Luther's voice filled the air as his dark wings erupted in fire above us sending embers to the ground. The snickering black smoke dispersed, skittering away in different directions.

Luther landed in front of me. His dark eyes glowed like molten embers.

"Friends of yours, Ifrit?" I asked.

"Ghouls," he said.

CHAPTER FIVE

Finley rushed out of the house after whatever binding spell the ghouls used dissipated. His sword was in hand, and Troy followed close behind with his pistol.

"What was it?" Finley asked.

"Ghouls," I repeated Luther's explanation.

"Bloody hell," Finley said. "Why are they here?"

"Said I have something they want," I said. "Kinda vague. What kind of spell was that?"

"Negation," Luther said. "They are the opposite of life. They take the life out of everything, even a home. They feed on it. If they are here, they are looking for a dead one they think we have."

"Winnie," I muttered.

"No," Levi said.

"It's the only thing that makes sense. Perhaps they think she belongs to the hereafter," I said.

"No, she is not of their kind," Luther said. "As far as I know, I'm the only one that is related to them here."

"You?" I asked.

"Ghouls are part of my kin. The nasty kin. The cousins you

hope never come to town because they will eat you out of house and home," he explained.

"Ew," I said.

"Exactly," Luther replied.

"Well, perhaps it's time I learn some of your mythology," I said.

Luther, Finley, and Troy moved back toward the house. I felt Levi's light touch on my arm. Looking up to him, I knew that he wasn't finished with our conversation, but we did what we always do. Push it aside. Save it for later.

"*We will finish this later,*" I said.

"*We will never be finished, Grace,*" he said.

I wrinkled my forehead at him. Levi had too many grand romantic notions. Not just the lovey-dovey kind either. These epic stories floating in his head of kingdoms and knights. It was the bard in him. He looked at everything through those eyes. Everything was a story to tell, but for me, I wasn't living a legendary story. I was just living. So was he, and he needed to see that side of it, too.

"Momma!" Winnie yelled running up to me. I bent down to her level as she wrapped her arms around my neck. "Don't leave me."

"Winnie, I'm not going anywhere. It would take a lot more than a few creepy smoke things to get me," I said.

I saw the pain in her eyes. Even though she'd inherited a buttload of power, she was still a 6-year-old girl. I was thankful that turning her into a fairy hadn't accelerated her growth. She would grow up normally, much like Levi had. I intended to take Luther up on his offer to work with her. She needed guidance, and the kind she needed, I couldn't give. Which put me into the being a momma and loving her department, and that was fine with me.

Looking around the room, I saw several people wiping tears from their eyes as Winnie held on to my neck without letting go. Astor started moving around the room asking people to exit to leave us to talk about the new visitors to Shady Grove.

Levi called Tennyson to make him aware of the ghouls and promised to report back to him whatever the war council talked about. We had formed the council before Dylan's death. It consisted of my knights: Levi, Troy, Tennyson, Astor, and Luther. Jenny was part of the group by default.

As the people filtered out of the house, Nestor took the children upstairs to get ready for bed. I hugged Aydan and told him I loved him. He moved his mouth, but no sound came out. I was beginning to wonder if he was going to be mute for all of his life.

"Goodnight, Little Bird," I said kissing his forehead before Nestor took him from me.

We settled down in the living room for Luther to tell us about the ghouls. Betty had stayed which was fine. I was thankful that Amanda left with Mark and the other wolf children that had come with them tonight. Astor returned from walking Ella to her car with a redness in his cheek. If he ever made the move, I was going to throw a goodbye party for his virginity.

"Alright, Ifrit. Talk," I said as Levi handed me a fresh glass of whiskey. He could calm me with a spell, but we had talked about his use of magic on me. It wasn't that I didn't trust him, but I didn't want that to be the default between us. I knew that the times he had forced his way with me that it had been with good reason.

"Ghouls are the children of Iblis. They sometimes take the form of the last human they devoured. Sometimes they shift to Hyenas," Luther explained.

"Oh, please, let them do that. I've got a pack that would love that fight," Troy said.

"It wouldn't be an easy win for the wolves," Luther warned.

"Even better," Troy responded.

"Ghouls are crafty. If they have come for someone, they will continue until they take what they have come for," Luther said.

"Who?" I asked.

Luther shifted in his seat uneasily. Betty dropped her eyes to the ground. They were keeping a secret. These people were important to me, and they knew that I wouldn't force them to tell it. Betty took a deep breath and nudged Luther.

"As you know, both of us have many children. When we got together after our spouses died, we combined our large families. There are thirteen children in all," Luther said.

"Are all of your children Ifrit?" I asked Luther.

"No, but they are all Jinn," he said. "I am cursed, therefore I am Ifrit."

"May I ask why you're cursed?"

"It is a long story but involves making many mistakes in my life. I was once a respected marid but fell. I would rather not speak of the details unless you command it," he said.

"Luther, you're my friend. I will not command it of you. I trust that if it has any bearing on our current situation, that you will divulge the information that I need to know. Otherwise, I just need to figure out why they are here. We have many other pressing matters," I said.

"Of course, Grace. I would never put you or Shady Grove in danger. I am thankful for the opportunity to set right the things I've done wrong," he said.

"Any suggestions on ousting them from here?" I asked.

"Yes, I have a friend that I can call. He specializes in dispatching them. A hunter of sorts," Luther said.

"Anyone we know?" Levi asked.

"Maybe. He's rather infamous," Luther smiled.

"He will fit right in," I smirked.

"I am not infamous," Astor interjected.

"Yes, you are Saint Cheeto," Levi countered.

Levi and Astor picked back and forth at each other as I watched the pained look on Betty's face. She wanted Luther to tell me more, but he shook his head. I loved them both and hoped that trusting them was the right thing to do.

"What kind of bard can't rhyme?" Astor said.

"I don't have to rhyme," Levi huffed. Astor had hit a sore point with my bard. I tried not laughing at either of them, but it was funny. "At least my pits aren't cherries and need to be popped."

"You've been looking at his pits?" I asked.

Levi's eyes twinkled with amusement. "Maybe. They are rather manly," Levi retorted.

"Stay away from my pits," Astor said seriously.

Levi winked at him, and I'm pretty sure that Astor shit in his pants. Betty's serious look finally cracked. Troy shook his head, then hid his face in his hands. Bless it. This was my war council. Except for Finley who had remained quiet through the whole exchange. While everyone laughed, I watched him across the room. He lifted his eyes to meet mine. We had both lost, but I had been the cause of his.

My spirit darkened. For at the moment that I snapped his wife out of existence, I knew it was the right thing to do, but I regretted it. He reassured me that I had done the right thing. His eye contact told me that even now, but he was my brother. I felt his despair. For all the years that we'd spent apart, then when he returned, I still felt like I was a million miles away from him. I needed him now more than ever, and our relationship needed a serious patch-up job.

"*Glory, stop blaming yourself,*" he said in my head.

"*I just want us to be better,*" I replied.

"*I'm as loyal to you as I have ever been. I'd give my life for you, Sister. Do not fear. This will pass,*" he said.

"*I love you, Fin,*" I said.

"*Love you, too. It's going to be fine,*" he tried to reassure me, but the pain was still there. I wasn't a stranger to pain. I knew what it looked like because it stared back at me in the mirror on a daily basis. Even though for months, I had tried to prepare myself for the worst when it came to Dylan, nothing could have prepared me for that inevitable loss.

"So, we call your hunter. Do you think he can get here soon?" I asked.

"If he is available, I suspect he will be in town tomorrow. With your permission, of course," Luther said.

"Of course. Please bring him to me so that I may meet him when he arrives," I said. "Now, since we are all here except for Tennyson, I want to know if any of you have suggestions on how to break our prisoner?"

"Let Jenny go a round with her," Finley suggested. He knew the capabilities of a grindylow.

"It is an option. I'd rather do it myself though," I said. "However, I admit to turning my face to my father's torture methods."

"I agree. Let Jenny and Tennyson take a crack at her," Levi said. "But I do have some more information on that front that I wanted to talk to you about."

"Why didn't you tell me?" I asked. Levi twitched in his seat. He didn't like me trying to call him out in front of everyone.

"Today wasn't about that," he muttered.

"Right. I'm sorry," I said. "We are here. Go ahead and tell us all."

He took a deep breath. "I spoke to someone about the red cloak. Apparently, there is an order known as the Order of the Red Cloak. They are a triad of fairy witches. Extremely powerful and well respected because of that power."

"Triad?" I said.

"Yes. There should be three of them patterned after the triple goddess. Crone, mother, and maiden," he explained. "I suspect Mable is the crone and Robin is the mother."

"That leaves the maiden," I said. "Is there another fairy witch in Shady Grove?"

"Not that I am aware of," Troy said.

"Me either," Luther replied.

"Order of the Red Cloak. They are ORCs," I said.

"Essentially," Levi said.

"We need to find the third," I said.

"She could be anywhere on the planet or under it," Levi said. "There is no way to know."

"No way to track them?" I asked.

"Not that I know of," he said.

"What about your contact? Would they know?" I asked.

"Um, I'm not sure," he replied, and I felt his mind shut off to me. I cocked my head sideways at the loss of his presence.

Locking eyes with him, I asked the question I shouldn't have. "Who is your contact?"

I knew by the mental block, he didn't want me to know. But by the wince on his face, I already regretted asking before he answered.

"Riley."

~

I opened and shut the door to the closet. All I needed was a whiff of the leather. It was like a damn drug. A Dylan Drug. My fix would never be fulfilled though, but no matter how desperate I got, that jacket was staying in that closet.

With a light tap on the door, Levi waited for me to call him into the room. After his admittance to discussing Mable with Riley, the meeting broke up. We decided to let everything rest until Luther's hunter showed up. Now he wanted to talk about it since it was just me and the children in the house. Astor left to be with Ella.

Levi had every right to talk to whomever he wanted. In fact, if he reformed his attachment to Riley, it was probably the best. I couldn't fathom how long my heart would be wrapped up in a dead phoenix. He grew impatient, and his forehead thumped against the door.

"Come in," I said.

When he came in, he wore a pair of pajama pants that hung low on his hips. No shirt. Ever since he showed his scars to me, he went back to his shirtless ways late at night and after showers. Scars or not, Levi was fairy fit. Lean muscles and beautiful lines. I couldn't help but to admire him as I always had. His scars drew me to him though. I think he knew that. Perhaps that's why he'd gone back to his bare chest bearing.

He closed the door behind him but didn't make eye contact with me. Closing the gap between us, I reached out to touch the scars around his sides. My fingers brushed over the ridges of the remnants of his fights with Dylan in the Otherworld. He had explained to me, that after the first fight he developed several spells to keep him from experiencing the burns again. He shivered as I touched the scars. It was the first time I'd touched them since he'd shown them to me.

A demented thought jumped into my head. His scars were like the leather jacket. A little piece of Dylan burned into his skin which was why I was touching them. I withdrew my hand with the thought, and his eyes shot to mine.

"It's okay. It doesn't hurt," he said.

"You know what I was thinking," I replied.

"Yes, and I'd do anything to give him back to you," he said.

I stepped back from him. "I'm sorry. I shouldn't have," I said.

"And I should have told you that I called Riley back after our confrontation at the diner," he said. "In my defense, I also called Tabitha hoping that she might know about the ORCs before I called Riley."

"You don't have to defend yourself with me," I said.

"I don't want Riley," he said.

"You don't have to want someone to be with them. Hell, I spent my life using men for what I wanted then kicking them to the curb. Just ask Joey Blankenship," I said.

"No need. Grace, you aren't that person anymore, and neither am I," he said.

"You never were," I said.

"Yes, I was. I tried Kady and Riley, but the fact of the matter was that neither one of them were you, and I knew that, but I did it anyway. I know that doesn't work, so it won't be happening again," he said.

"I just want you to be happy. You deserve it, and I'm not sure I'll ever have the capacity to give you what you want," I said.

A lopsided grin crossed his face. "Now, you're the idiot," he said.

"How dare you!" I said trying to be serious, but the grin persisted.

"That's right. You know my heart. As long as I'm here with you and the kids, I'm happy. I don't need or want anything else. If you kick me out, we will have issues, Queen," he smirked.

"Get out of my bedroom," I said pointing toward the door. "I will not stand by for this insolence."

"You better get used to it, because you're stuck with me," he said. I was so very stuck with him. I had been the moment he walked into my trailer. Fucking Jeremiah.

"Go to bed," I said pointing at the door.

He started to flirt back with me, but he held it inside. "We are solid. You said so," he said.

"Yes, we are," I replied.

"Then don't worry about Riley, or Kady, or anyone else," he said.

"Levi, go to bed," I pleaded. I didn't need to hear any more.

He backed away from me to the door. "Goodnight, Glory," he said.

"Don't call me that," I said.

I heard him laughing down the hallway to his room. After all the sadness and fear of the day, I went to bed with a smile, because my bard was exactly what I needed. And he fucking knew it.

CHAPTER SIX

As I unfolded the metal chair, Mable watched me intently with a smug look on her face. Was it bad that I wanted to see her squirm? She had no idea what I was capable of. She would think my father was a teddy bear compared to what I had planned for her red-cloaked ass. I had chosen a sweet sundress to wear. It was black but covered in a floral pattern. The days were turning colder, and I wanted to wear it one last time before I needed to break out the sweaters.

I sat down in the chair, crossing my legs like a proper lady.

"So good to see you, Gloriana," Mable said indicating my blonde hair and turquoise eyes. She had no idea that I hadn't reverted to my glamour since Dylan had died. I had a few questions as to how she obtained the jar. I wanted to know what she intended to accomplish by throwing the jar in the bonfire. I knew what the result had been. The death of my daughter. The death of my fiancé. Thankfully, Winnie was alive. It didn't lessen the wrath that seethed inside of me for Mable Sanders.

"Good morning, Mable," I said with a smile. "Is there anything I can get for you?"

"Oh, so diplomatic this morning. Aren't you sweet in your cute little dress? At least it is black, or are you finished mourning your fiancé already? I'm sure Levi is chomping at the bit," she said.

"Actually, I am," Levi said as he walked into the room. "But not for what you think, Mable."

"Oh, do tell. This should be interesting. I always loved soap operas," she said.

"I can't wait to see you get what is coming to you," he said, leaning on the wall next to me.

"You do realize that you can contain me on your own, right? You don't need the bard here to do it," she taunted.

The cell she was in was part of the old sheriff's department complex. We had taken turns at warding the cell, and she couldn't access power at all. She was a sitting duck.

"Oh, I'm not here to contain you. I'm just a spectator," I said.

"Really?" she laughed. "There is nothing you can do to make me talk."

"That's just it. I don't want you to talk. I want you to scream," I said as Tennyson and Jenny came into the cell block, locking the door behind them.

"Mable, it is so good to see you," Tennyson grinned as he cracked his knuckles.

"What are you doing here?" she spouted. "You can't interfere like this."

"I'm here to contain her," he said nodding to Jenny who shimmered to a muddy green color and slid through the jail cell bars with a squishing sound. "Oops! She got away."

Mable backed away from Jenny. "Ask me questions, Grace. I'll answer."

"I told you. I don't need you to talk. I already know that you're the crone in a triad of fairy witches known as the Order of the Red Cloak. You have no loyalties except for those of the mother and maiden. It is only a matter of time before I cut Robin's throat. I'm not sure who the maiden is, but I want to find out myself. You don't have to tell me," I said.

Jenny's arm turned into a glossy tentacle which reached across the cell wrapping itself around Mable's throat. Mable tried pulling it off of her, but Jenny tightened her hold.

"That is a thing of beauty," Tennyson said.

"*Weird tastes,*" Levi said.

"*To each his own,*" I replied.

"Please, Grace, I'll tell you anything," Mable gasped. "What will Nestor think of you torturing me?"

"He will be jealous. He wanted to do it himself," I said, standing up to walk to the bars of the cell. Her eyes bugged out of her head as Jenny held her tightly.

"Ask whatever you want, Grace. I'm willing to bet she will answer. If she doesn't, I've got seven more of these things that can find new cavities to explore," Jenny said with an evil glint in her eye. She was starting to scare me.

"*Fuck a duck,*" Levi said.

"*Give a whole new meaning to Hentai,*" I said. Levi started into a coughing fit, but I focused on Mable. I did have questions about the jar and Dylan.

"Why don't you just tell me things, and then I'll decide if they are good enough to let you die? Living is no longer an option for you, but the method of death will depend on what information you provide," I said.

"I left the fake jars for you around town," she exclaimed as Jenny formed another tentacle. It slithered up Mable's skirt wrapping around her calf. She stumbled but kept from hitting the floor.

"Already knew that," I said. I didn't exactly know, but I suspected it was her once she was caught.

The night of the bonfire, Mable was tackled by Astor who turned her over to Amanda and the wolves while I confronted Dylan with Winnie. They brought her here, and this was where she would stay until I had all the information I wanted.

"I don't work for Brockton. Neither does Robin," she said. "We serve a higher purpose."

"Oh, good. Now he can have a snake in the grass," I said. "What higher purpose?"

Jenny formed two more appendages which grabbed Mable's arms forcing her against the concrete block wall.

"We wish to see the veil between the worlds torn apart. Samhain is approaching. The veil thins. It is only a matter of time until all that is wild in the Otherworld slips through the barriers. I have a feeling some of them will be coming for you," she smiled, but only briefly. Jenny's noose tightened on her neck. Mable gasped for air.

"The wild do not dare cross en masse," I said.

She coughed and laughed at the same time. "You're a fool. There is no monarch to keep them in the Otherworld. Did you think your father's job consisted of fucking his concubines and drinking wine?"

I knew my father had duties in the Otherworld. The wild fairies respected my father and abided by his wishes. Mable was right. My father wasn't there to stop them from charging through the veil and wreaking havoc among the humans. But she was also wrong because I would stop them.

"Jenny, have your fun. Just don't kill her, yet," I said as I stood up to leave.

"Thank you, my Queen," Jenny grinned. Her golden teeth sparkled under the fluorescent lights. Tennyson bowed to me as I passed him with Levi on my heels.

"Grace, wait! Please! Don't leave me here with her. I beg you for mercy," Mable pleaded.

"I'm not in a merciful mood at the moment, Mable. Unless you're ready to spill your guts," I said without looking at her.

"It was Robin's idea to throw the jar in the fire. We thought he would kill Levi! Winnie wasn't supposed to get hurt," she exclaimed.

"That's your defense? Robin did it? I'm not an idiot, Mable. I understand the power of the three. There isn't anything Robin can make you do without your consent. Don't piss on my leg and tell me it's raining," I said while walking out the door.

She started to speak again, but it mixed with an awful sounding garble. I didn't tell Jenny to leave her where she could speak, perhaps I should have specified. Too late now. The scary part of the whole confrontation and walking out of that room knowing that

Jenny was going to have fun playing with her was that I didn't care. She had deceived this entire town, my father, my grandfather, and my family. She sat in on private meetings because my father considered her a trusted servant. She could rot for all I cared.

I wanted to rip her limbs off and beat her with them. A dusting wouldn't do. It just wasn't enough for the pain and heartache she had caused. She was a villain. A betrayer. My anger swelled up inside of me as we stepped outside of the old jail.

Suddenly Levi's arms surrounded me as he muttered, "Office."

We appeared in my office which was actually a trailer. I jerked away from him.

"What the hell are you doing?" I spat.

"You need to calm down," he said. His eyes focused on me, and his face tightened. He wasn't afraid of me at all. At the moment, I thought that was a bad thing. I could rip him apart with a few words. "No, you can't."

"Dare me," I said with a growl.

He grabbed my wrist, dragging me through the main room into the bedroom where my desk was, then further into the bathroom. Spinning me around to look at the mirror, I jerked back involuntarily from the mirror. Looking down at my hands, I saw that they were blue and transparent like ice. My face was pale, and my lips had turned deep purple like a frozen corpse.

The blue swirls on my skin pulsed with power. All of this was happening, and I didn't feel it at all. I felt no different save the anger inside of me toward Mable. Levi's hand slid down my arm to my wrist, resting above my tattoo. He didn't play music, but I could feel the calming spell radiating out of him into me. I watched myself in the mirror as my normal complexion returned. I lifted my left hand to see the ice fading away.

"Shit," I muttered.

Levi's breath brushed through my hair as he spoke, "You never have to worry about going too far. I'm here, and I won't let you."

"I don't need a babysitter," I said, but it had no fire behind it.

"No, you don't. You need a bard," he said. I could hear the smile on his face without looking at him. I dared to meet his eyes in the mirror. His cobalt eyes stared back at me. For a moment, I could see the power in them as if I were hypnotized.

I gasped pulling my hand away from him. Burying my face in my hands, the bravado left me, and I shook with the realization that I had tumbled off the edge that I had walked for so long. The evil inside of me had welled up and poured over. I remembered this part of me vividly now. I remembered being so angry at Finley once that I struck him with my icy hand, breaking his jaw.

Levi stepped between me and the mirror, leaning on the vanity. He pulled me to him, and I didn't protest or try to stop him.

"I'm sorry," I said into his chest.

"You have nothing to worry about with me. You know that. No apology needed," he said.

"I've been like this before. I remember it now," I said.

"It comes with being part of the Unseelie," he said.

"I deserved to be banished from the Otherworld," I said.

"No more than anyone else, Grace. You were a pawn in a game played between your father and Morgana. Now you're the Queen. The most powerful piece on the board," he said. "Like that? A chess reference. Bet you didn't know I can play chess?"

"Your abilities never cease to amaze me," I said as my mood changed. Levi wasn't using magic now. He was just being himself.

"There is more where that came from," he teased.

"I have no doubt," I said.

"One day I'll show you," he said turning confident.

"In your wildest dreams," I said pushing myself away from him. I had always flirted with Levi, but now it made me uncomfortable.

"You have no idea how wild," he grinned.

"Please," I scoffed. "Fairy."

"Grace." His voice became sober.

"Huh?"

"I'll always bring you back if it is needed, but one day, you are going to have to unleash that thing inside of you. Don't be afraid to be who you are," he said.

Your true self.

Levi was working on a theme now. "What's your point, Dublin?"

"Just that I know as do you that to be Queen of the Otherworld, especially the Unseelie side, that things might get nasty. You might have to do things you wouldn't normally do like torture a servant. I want you to know that I stand behind you no matter what you do as long as you're being true to yourself," he said.

I pondered his words before responding. Levi wasn't giving me a pass to be ruthless and brutal. He was giving me the support I needed for when times called for the more distasteful parts of ruling. I had tasted those times with the snap of my finger. Extinguishing lives in the Vale. I gave him the only response I could muster because the truth was the darkness inside of me still scared me, and I wasn't ready to accept it.

"I'd rather you stand beside me than behind me," I said.

"Same difference," he shrugged.

"No, it isn't," I replied. "If you want me to admit it, I will. I need you, Levi. I can't do this without you. For all the fronting, I'm still afraid of myself, and you're that safety blanket that I know will point me in the right direction. I had two, but Dylan is gone now."

"You can do it yourself. I don't want to be a crutch. Which if you think about it, is technically beside you, but you still depend on it to walk. You don't need me to do what you do. I know my place here, and I don't think you get it sometimes," he said. "I'm not a safety net. I'm your cheerleader."

"I bet you'd look good in a skirt," I smirked.

"I look good in anything," he said. Damn. He was getting bold. Or perhaps, he was finally feeling more like himself after the events in the Otherworld.

"And nothing," I said, then clasped my hand over my mouth. "I did not say that!"

"Yes, you did," he laughed. I was thankful he kept his distance. My emotions were a big swirling mess. Between the cold hatred for Mable Sanders and the ORCs, the confusion overtaking the right actions as a leader, the grief over Dylan, and the impending disaster of my emotions for Levi, I was a wrecking ball waiting to be unleashed. I just hoped I hit the right wall on the first swing.

CHAPTER SEVEN

"Momma, I love Mr. Luther," Winnie proclaimed at the dinner table.

"That's great. What is he teaching you?" I asked.

"Lots of things," she said.

"Like?" Levi asked.

She sneered at him. "Wynnona Riggs, manners, please," I scolded.

"*I shouldn't have asked,*" Levi said.

"*You didn't do anything wrong. She's got to learn control. Not just of the fire, but of her emotions,*" I said.

"*She is a child,*" Levi said.

"*Which makes it more difficult, but not any less important,*" I returned.

"Yes, ma'am," she muttered. "We are working on using my fire a little at a time. He lined up some dried leaves on a table, and I had to just set one of them on fire instead of burning them all." She lined up small pieces of lettuce as she told her story, pointing at each one as she talked.

"How did that go?" I asked.

"Not very well the first three times, but by the fourth time, I didn't burn the table. Still working on just burning one leaf," she said as she chomped down on a taco.

"Just take your time, Winnie. Your father gave you an important gift. I'm sure you will make a great phoenix," I said.

"Or she will burn the town down," Astor interjected.

"Astor!" I exclaimed. Levi laughed.

"I will not!" Winnie protested, but she giggled.

"You might. Fiery little one," Astor said winking at her.

"Maybe just a few buildings," she laughed.

"I'm pretty sure I'd lose my job if you did that," I said.

"Nah, Momma, you will always be the Queen," she said.

"Hear! Hear!" Astor said lifting his sweet tea glass. Winnie lifted hers and they touched them together. Levi joined them in the toast. Aydan who sat in a high chair next to the table smearing mashed potatoes over his tray stopped to clap with potatoes between his fingers. I closed my eyes to push back the tears. Dylan should be here for moments like this, but he wasn't. When I opened my eyes, everyone continued to laugh and talk, but Levi's face lost the joy of the moment. I shook my head to brush it off, then joined back into the conversation about Winnie learning to use her powers.

She kissed both of her keys before taking off her necklace and laying it beside her bed.

"Are we still having a birthday party?" she asked.

"Yes, of course," I said. "Do you still want unicorns?"

"Duh!" she said with a smile.

"Then we shall have unicorns," I replied. "We will do it this weekend. Is that alright with you little Phoenix?"

"Yes, ma'am. Momma, I know I wanted to be a fairy like everyone else, but it's not all it's cracked up to be," she said.

"Ain't that the truth," I laughed. "But your daddy thought you could do it."

"I'll make him proud," she said with the confidence of a child.

"I'm already proud of you," I replied.

"Are you?" she asked.

"Of course, Winnie. One day you will learn to control the gifts that were given to you. I believe in you," I answered.

"Thank you, Momma. Did Daddy go away so I could stay here?" she asked. She had asked the question before, but I think sometimes she just needed to be reassured that he made the decision to take her place. As if, perhaps she had done something wrong. She hadn't, of course, but sometimes I couldn't understand the mind of a child. Especially Winnie.

"Yes, Daddy gave up his life for yours," I said. "He wanted to do it because he loved you so much."

"I figured he did. It would take a lot of love to give up your life for your daughter," she said. "He let me live, and he gave me his power, too. Makes him the best Daddy ever."

Suddenly, I felt as if a semi had plowed over me. The best Daddy ever gave up his life and power to save his daughter. Had she died within the Vale, she would not have returned. For Winnie, that was Dylan. For me, it was a king.

"Yes, it does," I responded as I kissed her on the forehead. "Goodnight, Winnie."

"Night, Momma," she said.

I quietly left the room, then dashed down the hallway to my room. Shutting the door behind me, I gasped in the realization that since my father's death I had varying degrees of hatred for him for lying to me. However, the fact was that he had done exactly what Dylan did for Winnie. Exactly. And I was an ungrateful child. How did I thank him now? Just march out there and tell him. I hadn't been to see him since Dylan died.

Closing my eyes, I felt the power of the stone circle in the forest just beyond my home. I needed to see my father.

When I opened my eyes, I stood just inside the ring of stones. As I approached the center stone, it glowed, coming to life. My father's ghostly blue form floated above the stone.

"I am so sorry, Gloriana. I know that you loved Dylan," he said.

"I love you, Daddy," I whimpered.

He looked puzzled for a moment, then returned the sentiment.

"I love you, too, Daughter. Come speak to me. You have something to say?"

"I do," I said, walking up to the center stone.

"You may say whatever you wish to say. I want to hear whatever it is," he smiled.

"Thank you for giving your life up for me. For giving me your power and knowledge," I said. "Although I'm only getting a little bit of the knowledge as I need it, but thank you. Now, I understand now the sacrifice you made for me. Dying here in the Vale."

"What brought this on?" he asked. "Not that I'm not thankful, but something stirred this inside of you."

"Winnie. She's the Phoenix now," I said.

"Bloody hell, you say?" he swore. "How did that happen?"

"She died, so he claimed her as his heir. I gave her a piece of the fruit from the tree, and a vial of water from the fountain, then he gave her his powers. She rose while he faded into nothing," I said as tears rolled down my cheeks.

"Gloriana, I'm so sorry about Serafino," he said.

"No, wait. That's not all. I've been blind thinking that you gave me your kingdom because you thought I'd do a better job than you. That allowing me to be banished made me into a different kind of fairy so that I could do things differently. I'm a fool to believe it was anything more than a parent sacrificing his life for his child like Dylan did for Winnie. I've been arrogant," I said.

He stepped from the stone and his form coalesced into something more solid. Lifting his palm to my cheek, I felt my father's touch. He was almost completely whole standing there with me.

"I wish I could say that I had that kind of foresight. You're welcome to use that as the story. Makes me out to be wiser than I really am," he smiled. "But yes, Gloriana, I gave my life up simply because I didn't want my child to die. However, I do believe in you. I think that my brother needs to be very careful. Hopefully, his days are numbered."

"They are," I said. "I just haven't counted them out yet."

He laughed, then cut his eyes to the edge of the circle. I knew who was there. My shadow. "He hasn't stepped into the role yet?" Father asked.

"I'm not ready for that, and neither is he. He's the one that had to do it. I couldn't kill him," I replied. "It's only been a few months."

"Maybe so, but your heart started to pound harder when he arrived. The connection between the two of you is undeniable," he observed.

"You have not been very gracious to him," I countered.

"No one will ever be good enough for you in my eyes," he smiled. I leaned on his hand. I could feel it. Just a slight tingle. "What is this about the knowledge? What did you say?"

"That I remember or know things when it comes time to need them. Like I suddenly knew the spell to turn Winnie into a fairy just as it was needed, but not before. I suppose your knowledge would be too overwhelming for me to take all at once," I said.

"Gloriana, I haven't bestowed my knowledge on you at all. Other than what you gained the moment I died," he revealed.

"But I know things right when I need them," I said.

"That is your own knowledge. I believe that because you spent so much time away from the Otherworld that you forgot all the things you can do. From the moment you stepped back into the Otherworld with Levi when you were investigating Demetrius Lysander, your knowledge has returned bit by bit. Gloriana, you don't need anything else from me to rule," he replied.

"Then why are you still here?" I asked.

A wind swirled inside the circle, and Levi appeared at my side. A cool breeze followed by a warm gust. It repeated several times until Lilith stood on the center stone. Pregnant and barefoot. However, she wore a dress much like the one I wore in Summer. She looked like what you expect of a goddess. My father bowed at the waist to her, and Levi copied his motion. I hadn't bowed to her before, but I supposed I should since I knew who she was now. I lowered my head until she spoke.

"Sometimes life doesn't give us enough time to say what needs to be said," she said. Her voice filled the circle, bouncing off the outer stones, then echoing back to us. "Oberon needed to know his daughter loved him, and you needed to realize that you did. Humility isn't your strong point, Gloriana."

Levi snorted, and I swatted at him. "So, he was here simply so I could tell him I loved him?"

"And you needed to know that you can do this on your own. Even for all the times you've said it, you needed to know that *your* knowledge and *your* power is capable. You need no one or nothing else," she said. "Whether you complete your task isn't up to me, but I felt like your Father deserved this moment for all the years he honored me and the tree. Your trouble isn't over, Gloriana, but you are ready."

"Is Dylan with you?" I asked.

"His spirit lives within the tree," she said.

"He's okay?" I asked.

"It's hard to explain, but in terms that you would understand, his soul is at peace," she said. She lifted her eyes to Levi. "Levi Rearden, worry not for you did as you were asked to do. You have a role in all of this too. I look forward to seeing it develop."

"Thank you, ma'am," he said.

"Your mother's spirit is a strong one. I see it living inside of you," she said.

"I miss her," he replied.

"Everyone misses their dead. Honor them, but remember that they live on inside of you," she instructed. "Come now, King. It is time to go."

"No!" I exclaimed. "Please don't take him now." Levi moved closer to me but didn't reach out to touch me.

"Gloriana, we have been afforded more time than we deserved. I love you. Go out there and take it back from him. It's yours, and he will not rest until you and your brother are dead," he said.

"Finley!" I called out into the darkness.

My brother appeared on the edge of the ring of stones in the same spot that Levi had appeared. He ran in a sprint to where we stood.

"Father?" he said.

"My son. Stand by her," Oberon demanded.

"Yes, Father. As always," Finley responded. "Are you leaving?"

"It is time," Oberon said.

"Go unto our ancestors. Take the hand of the goddess and find peace on the other side," Finley replied as his eyes welled up with tears.

"Goodbye, my children," he said with a smile. "You have already made me proud."

He stepped back up on to the stone next to the pregnant Lilith. She smiled as they faded away. The night turned cold, and the dew on the grass froze around our feet. The light blue particles that remained of my father's image approached me. Finley and Levi stepped back as my tattoo ignited with silvery threads coursing over my limbs. The blue dust settled into my skin, and the lines of power pulsed a ghostly blue.

My casual clothes disappeared, and a long black dress covered my body. My single horn crown appeared on my head. A far-off voice proclaimed, "This is my daughter, Gloriana. She is the Queen of Winter and the Vale."

Finley and Levi bowed down to one knee. Finley lowered his head, but Levi stared into my eyes. I knew what he was thinking.

Your true self.

"Please get up," I pleaded. Finley laughed as he stood. "You didn't seem sad to see him go."

"I've been out to speak with him multiple times. I knew he was only here for a short while. We were lucky to have him for this long," he said. "You look beautiful, Sister."

"Thank you, but I don't feel different," I muttered.

"I don't think you're supposed to feel different," he said. "Thank you for calling for me. I need to get back to what I was doing."

"What or who?" I asked.

He grinned. "Who."

He disappeared leaving me alone in the circle with Levi.

"Are you okay?" he asked.

"It was unexpected, but I feel like I said my piece," I said. "Finley is right. He was only here for a short time. I knew that."

"Doesn't make it any easier, Grace," Levi replied.

"Do you want me to cry?" I asked.

"I want you to be honest with me," he answered.

"I will store it away along with everything else, Levi," I said.

"You're not just beautiful like this. You look strong. I feel the strength and power inside of you. You once told me that I didn't need to be afraid of my power, but I can say the same thing back to you. Don't be afraid. Don't hold back," he said. His words were impassioned. I wanted to kick myself for all the times I pushed him. The roles were reversed now.

"I can't take back Winter without the fourth stone," I pondered.

"Then we call upon the Lady of the Lake and ask for permission to use it," he suggested.

"I had to show force with the Sylph. Dylan didn't give the fire to me until he saw me fight the Sylph. Lilith only gave me the earth stone after the test at the tree. I'm sure there will be some rite of passage," I said.

"We should go home," Levi insisted. "I'll see what I can find out about Nimue tomorrow."

"I want to do it tonight," I continued.

"Grace, no. You need to go home. It's been a long day," he said.

"Don't start demanding things from me. You have no right," I snarled. My emotions were teetering on the edge. The tattoos on my body flared with my anger. Levi didn't flinch. Little bastard.

"You can be as angry with me as you want, but you need to go home. Let this sink in before you make a mistake," he said.

"You're getting on my ever-loving nerves, Levi Rearden!" I shouted.

"Because I'm right," he said smugly.

"Fuck off," I exclaimed in frustration. Gathering my power, I jumped to the house. I felt him jump right behind me.

My conscious kicked in scolding me for treating him that way simply because I knew I could. Levi was the tail end of my anger too many times. My emotions flipped back and forth. Before I wouldn't even have considered apologizing. Now I wasn't just mad, I was mad at myself.

"Grace," he said calling out to me. I ignored him as I stomped into the house, but then suddenly I remembered my sleeping children. I stopped before I made too much noise. Waving my hand, the black dress, crown, and skin adornments disappeared. I stood once again in my jeans and t-shirt.

Levi slipped in the front door behind me, closing it gently. He brushed past me taking two steps at a time.

"Levi," I called out to him.

"Goodnight, Gloriana," he said, then shut me out of his head.

CHAPTER EIGHT

Levi

I TOSSED AND TURNED ALL NIGHT, AS I HAD SINCE THE NIGHT DYLAN died. It didn't matter that I knew it was coming. I couldn't have prepared myself for the pain that I experienced along with the feed-back of grief and pain from Grace. Being connected to her as I was, I felt everything she felt plus my own. It wasn't as if I was taking it from her either. Nope. We were just both living it. I didn't have the heart to tell her that I felt it.

So, tonight, when she pitched her fit, I cut her out of my head. I thought that if I turned it off for just one night I could sleep. I couldn't have been more wrong. Knowing that she was at home attempting to rest, gave me some sort of peace, but with her cut off, I didn't know whether she had left the house or not. I also couldn't let her lash out at me. I refused to be her whipping boy.

The complication in all of it was that I loved her, and whether she admitted it or not, she loved me too. Fuck Dylan's dream. I had always felt like she was meant to be mine. I endured living in the house with them until I couldn't anymore, but the moment I stepped back into Shady Grove from my captivity in the Other-world, I knew that eventually, she would be mine.

In those moments as I raced across town trying to find her, all I cared about was her. Since then, I'd found my desires were divided. Winnie and Aydan were like my own children. My urge to protect them didn't come from Dylan's request that I should, it came from my own heart. I'd loved Winnie for a long time, and Aydan was growing on me.

My attentions were also needed in the town. With the ward up, I felt every fairy that entered and exited the town. We hadn't had any incursions by humans since the ward went up, but I would feel that too. I wanted to see the people inside the Vale live a good life. A long one without the looming threat of eternal death. I'd searched the book looking for ways to break the curse, but I hadn't found anything yet. No matter how much I memorized it, what I was looking for wasn't there.

The songbook wasn't the authority on magic though. It was just the authority on bard magic. I was part fairy, so I had inherent abilities beyond the gift Oberon had given me. Those abilities had never been developed, but I felt them. I felt the cold of winter when Grace was the platinum blonde covered in shining tattoos. That power made me more powerful. I supposed a lot of that had to do with the blood bond between us. It wasn't what I had intended, but she honored me by sharing the bond.

I had offered myself as her servant, but I was glad that I wasn't. More than anything, I wanted her to see me as her equal. Not because I wanted to be with her, but because I knew we could defeat anything that came our way as long as we were together.

Shutting her out tonight hurt me. So, I know that it hurt her too. I knew that she lashed out at me because of the grief and pain she held inside, but she needed to know that I wouldn't just roll over and take it. She would apologize. I hoped she would apologize. I didn't know for sure if she would or not.

Dragging myself out of bed before dawn, I took a shower. Staring down at the scars covering my torso, I winced at the memory of their pain. I could glamour them, but I wanted that

CHAPTER 8 | 53

constant reminder that if I let my guard down, I could be hurt. Unfortunately, that went for Grace, too. She could ruin me in an instant. Hell, she had already ruined my heart.

I dried off and dressed for the day. No parading around in a towel today. I'd have to take my medicine after shutting her out. I loved the way she looked at me when I did it, but I knew that the fairy inside of her desired me as a sexual object. I wanted more, and until she was ready to give it, no more towel parades.

I slipped down the steps silently so I wouldn't wake the children. I found a bowl and a box of sugary cereal in the kitchen. Pouring some milk over the cereal, I watched out the back window of the house as the sun started to rise. A light fog hung over the ground. When I turned around from the kitchen counter, I realized she was sitting in the recliner across the room. Her bright turquoise eyes watched me closely.

"Good morning," I muttered. I had been strong all night and hadn't let her back in. But seeing her there, staring at me, I wanted to open my mind to her. I craved that cold stirring when we connected.

"Why?" she asked. When I met Grace, she avoided the tough questions. She always knew what was going on around her by observing, but now, after all that had happened, she didn't hold back.

Taking slow bites of the cereal, I formulated my response. I didn't want it to seem petty although in a way, it was, I had to have some dignity. She wouldn't respect me if I constantly gave into her.

"I know that you're in pain, and the thing you said to me you didn't mean. But, I won't allow you to take it out on me," I said. When I moved over to the couch, I realized she was still wearing the same clothes from the night before. "Did you sit here all night?"

"Yes," she said. Damn. She knew how to break my resolve. I didn't know if she was doing it on purpose, or if she didn't realize how much one small word would affect me.

"You need rest. For your children. For the town," I said.

"So do you," she said.

"I'm fine," I replied.

"Are you?" she asked. She knew I wasn't. "Don't lie to me, Levi."

"I've never lied to you," I shot back too quickly.

"Don't start now," she said.

I sat the cereal bowl down on the coffee table and ran my hands through my wet hair. "I feel your pain. I feel your grief. Not just mine, but yours too. It can be overwhelming."

"Do you think the connection is one way?" she asked.

Of course, it wasn't. She felt my pain too. "No," I answered.

"I would rather feel your pain along with mine, than not feel you at all," she said.

That was as close to an apology as I ever expected to get from her. "You shouldn't have to," I said.

"Are you protecting me from you or you from me? Because it's hard to tell," she said.

"I just didn't like the way you dismissed me, Grace. I can handle the pain and grief of losing Dylan. I can handle your pain and grief too. What I can't handle is you disrespecting me. I know I am a convenient target for your wrath. You know that no matter what you say to me, I'm not leaving. Not ever. But you can't use that as an excuse to say whatever the hell you want," I said. I probably said too much.

For the first time since I noticed her sitting there, she turned her eyes from me. In the dim light of dawn, I saw a tear roll down her cheek. She didn't wipe it away. She ignored it. I wanted to wipe it away for her.

"Maybe we both need to learn to function without using each other as a crutch," she said.

"Do you think I make you weak?" I asked.

"You're a distraction, Levi. My focus needs to be on the town and my children. I can't continuously worry about your feelings for me," she said.

"You shouldn't worry about my feelings. I haven't changed how I approach you. Nothing has changed between us. I've made sure of that. I know I flirt sometimes, but I did that when he was alive. I did it knowing he could bust me in the face for it, but it's just me being me. You're right. Our focus should be on the kids and the town. Whether you believe me or not, that is what I care about, but I can't focus on those things without focusing on you. In all the pieces to this puzzle, you are the centerpiece. None of it works without you. If you feel like I'm focusing on you, it's because I am. Not for myself, but for the things that matter the most," I said. "Forgive me, if I thought you should rest instead of going off half-cocked to summon the Lady of the Lake."

"I'm not sure I can be half-cocked. I'm pretty sure that's physically impossible," she said, making light of the conversation. I had reached her limit of comfort. Now she would deflect the seriousness.

"Not like a dick, Grace. Like a shotgun," I said. Her mind was perpetually in the gutter.

"Oh," she replied.

Leaning forward, I put my elbows on my knees and folded my hands in front of my face. Power moved in the room, and I felt her sitting beside me. My resolve weakened. At any moment, I would let her back in. I couldn't help myself.

"Look at me," she whispered.

I clenched my teeth. She knew how to get to me. She knew my weaknesses. She was my weakness. Looking up to her, I was caught off-guard. She reached up to the scar on my face, tracing it from my forehead to my chin. Her cool touch should have frozen my heart, but instead, it melted in her hands once again. I caught her hand before she lowered it. Bringing it to my lips, I kissed the inside of her palm.

Then she said the one thing I never expected her to say.

"You were right, Levi. I'm sorry," she said. The immature male inside of me jumped up and down and gave himself a high five. I was glad that one wasn't doing the talking.

"I have no choice but to forgive you," I said.

"You better," she replied.

I released the block on my mind. She sighed. Instead of searching my brain to see if I was being truthful with her, she pulled back from me.

"I think I'll go lay down," she said.

"I'll get the kids. You rest," I said.

"You haven't slept either," she said.

"Yes, but I'm younger than you. I can take it," I said.

I knew better than to comment on a woman's age, but I did it anyway. Part of me loved pushing her buttons. Her nostrils flared. I was waiting on her routine comeback, but instead, she shook her head, then climbed the stairs to her room.

CHAPTER NINE

GRACE

SITTING BACK IN A LAWN CHAIR WHILE SIPPING ON AN ORANGE SODA, I watched the new daily routine of Astor Knight, along with my brother, who refused to pick a last name. They sparred. With swords. I told them both it was utterly ridiculous because I doubted that we would need swords in this fight. But as Astor reminded me, the fight in Summer included a great many swords. They were just 'staying in shape.'

Ella sat next to me watching the ginger knight. I couldn't rightly call him my knight anymore. It was very clear to see that he belonged to her. She took this moment to clarify that for me.

"Do you have any intentions toward Astor?" she asked.

"No, why?" I responded.

"Because I want him," she said.

"I'm pretty sure you have him already," I said.

"He's not giving in," she explained. I giggled.

"You know in this life he's a virgin. He might need a little help," I said.

"It's not that. I've tried everything. Trust me! He won't give in," she said.

"Did you ask him why?"

"He says that after a proper courtship, he will ask my father to marry me. Then, and only then, will he give it up," she said.

"Noble," I said with a smile.

"Frustrating," she said.

"That too," I agreed.

"How long is a proper courtship?" I asked.

"He says at least a year," she groaned.

I laughed. "I could interfere," I said.

"No, don't force him," she said.

"Ella, I would never. He just needs the proper encouragement," I said. "If you don't mind, I'll give it a try."

"Please," she finally agreed.

"What happens if he decides to wait despite my persuasion?" I asked.

"Then I will wait," she said.

"Good answer," I replied.

We sat in silence watching the two knights parry back and forth. Both were accomplished swordsmen, but Astor was the better of the two. I figured that was because Finley always found a distraction instead of practicing when we were younger. I even took a few lessons in swordplay per my father's demand, but it bored me. I had no desire to fight with a sword. Which brought me back to this impending war. I hoped my magical gifts were enough.

The low rumble of a Harley came from the direction of the main road. Levi had gone to town to meet up with Tennyson and Jenny to get an update on their efforts with our prisoner. He had already told me through our connection that they didn't get anything new out of her. He also spoke to Luther who said his hunter was delayed in arriving. I hoped that we could find more information about what the ghouls wanted, but we hadn't come up with anything.

The connection we shared he had cut off a few nights ago. I hated to admit it, but it was agony. Levi was my security blanket. I felt safe when we were connected. He drove up on the Harley without a helmet on. I scowled at him. He just smiled knowing my protest. He assured me that whenever he drove it, that he charged up his tattoo, and kept the music flowing so that he could use it in a moment's notice. I still didn't trust the damn thing. It's my own fault because I bought the motorcycle for him last Christmas. He had gone back to driving it around more often after Dylan's death. I was probably being a little overprotective. He was more likely to get killed in Shady Grove by a rogue ogre than by crashing his motorcycle.

"This looks like fun," he said. "I think I'll try."

"Don't hurt yourself, Dublin," I said.

He walked over to the two knights, exchanged a few words, and Finley offered him his sword. Astor walked through some basic steps with him. I felt him charging his magic. He could use all the magic he could muster, but unless he had some skill with the sword, Astor would beat him easily.

"*If he beats me, you can kiss my wounds,*" he smirked.

"*Keep dreamin', Dublin,*" I said.

"*Then you can kiss the victor.*" A grin crossed his face, and if it weren't completely adorable, I would have slapped him.

"He's talking to you," Ella said, observing the way I narrowed my eyes at him.

"Yes, we are very connected. Too connected sometimes," I said.

"I know that he's been with other women, but as far as I could tell, he's only ever wanted you," she said.

"No. I don't think so." She was right, but I wasn't admitting that. "We share a close bond, and I'm thankful that he is a part of my family's life."

"But…" she said.

"But my fiancé just died, and my heart doesn't function properly anymore. He deserves better," I said. Unsure of why I was spilling my guts to her, I decided that I wouldn't say any more on the subject.

"It's not my business, and I've got little to no experience with love matters, but from my perspective, loving Levi has nothing to do with Dylan," she said.

"Then we have very different perspectives," I said, knowing I should have never pursued the conversation with her. Loving Levi had nothing to do with Dylan, and everything to do with just not being capable of that deep emotion. When I gave in to Dylan, I had no idea how much his love would reach my heart. I'd never thought it possible, and when it did touch me, I jumped in heart first. Now I was just floundering. My focus was on Shady Grove, which I had resolved to do when Levi shed his button up plaid shirt, sporting a black "wife-beater" underneath. My focus suddenly switched to the changeling bard that had apparently been working out more often.

"Wow!" Ella said.

"Wow, indeed," I grumbled. Levi stretched his arms with that devilish glint in his eye. He knew what I thought of him, but there were two beautiful women staring at him. Ella looked to the ground then back up at Astor.

"Tell him to take his shirt off too. Then we can gawk at both of them," I said.

"Astor is hairy," she said.

"Nothing wrong with a hairy chest," I said.

"Nothing at all," she grinned. "I just want to see the rest of it."

"Astor, if you hurt him," I warned the experienced knight.

"I'll go easy on him, My Queen. I understand that he is only a poet. I'll make sure to keep his tattoo arm safe," Astor taunted.

"Keep talking, you overgrown, hairy carrot," Levi teased back.

"Ready up, Bard," Astor said raising his sword.

"Whenever you're ready, Copper Nob," Levi said bringing Finley's sword up to a middle ready stance. I noticed his hand positions and his stance. They were identical to the starting position that Finley used. Maybe I knew a little more about sword fighting that I admitted, but it's because I used to watch my father's knights practice. Taking my eyes off Levi, I turned to Finley who grinned.

"What?" he said.

"Exactly. What?" I said.

"Maybe he's just a natural," Finley shrugged.

"Riiiiiight," I said dragging out the vowel.

The sound of swords clanging together brought my attention back to the fighters. Astor withdrew his sword from Levi's defensive position, then lunged forward. Levi jumped to the side swinging his sword downward toward Astor's legs. Astor planted his sword in the ground just as Levi's strike got close to him deflecting the strike. He jerked the sword up out of the ground swinging it around toward Levi who had gotten off balance. I jumped to my feet as I watched Astor's gleaming sword sweep down toward Levi. When I started to interfere, Finley jerked me to the side.

"No," he growled.

My eyes darted back to Levi who had lifted his sword to a hanging left position causing Astor's strike to slide down his blade. Now the ginger knight was off-kilter, giving Levi the advantage. Instead of using his sword, Levi lifted a black boot then shoved Astor in the ass to the ground. The knight grunted, rolling over to deflect a half-hearted final blow by Levi.

"Yield!" Levi yelled.

"I yield," Astor muttered.

I stood frozen staring at the two of them. They were laughing as Levi helped him up off the ground. Astor patted him on the back.

"You've gotten much better," Astor said.

"Thanks. I've had a good teacher," Levi replied as he looked back to me.

"Grace, are you okay?" Ella asked.

"Um, yeah," I said not taking my eyes off Levi. She giggled, then rushed over to Astor who hugged her. She kissed him which drew a deep red blush to his cheeks.

"She's in shock," Finley said.

"No, I'm not," I muttered.

Levi walked over handing the sword to Finley. He reached up to peel my hand from in front of my gaping mouth. I hadn't even realized I was standing there like that.

"When did you? What in the world? How?" I said unable to complete a sentence.

"I'm good," he said.

"Yes," I replied. "But how?"

"Practice," he replied.

I felt the tingle of his power rush up my arm from where he still held my hand. "You?" I asked looking at Finley.

"Nope," Finley grinned. "He chose the best as his teacher."

I looked over to Astor and Ella who were arm in arm. Astor shook his head at me.

"Who?" I said looking back at Levi.

"Tennyson," he replied.

"He always was the best, the wanker," Astor said.

"Why? You have plenty of power without this," I mumbled.

Finley pulled away from us, joining Astor and Ella as they went into the house. Levi squeezed my hand. "If this comes to war, which it is going to, I need to be ready for anything. After Dylan died, I asked Tennyson to show me a few things. When we have our meetings about the progress of the town and when he gives me info about the Otherworld, he teaches me," he said.

"I don't want you fighting like this," I said.

"Grace, I'm going to fight like the rest of them. I'll fight better than them, because of my magic," he said. "And if I die…"

"Stop!" I said. "No." I jerked my hand away from him and walked toward the house. He blinked in front of me. "Move it or lose it!"

"No, Grace, you stop!" he said with power behind it. Enough to hold me still for a moment.

"I am going to bust your ass if you don't let me go," I said grinding my teeth.

"I am going to fight beside you, beside them, and I will do whatever it takes to make sure we win this war," he said. "You can't protect me."

"The hell I can't," I said.

"Unfortunately, you don't have a choice. We are equal. You did that. Not me. Release," he said.

Heaving a long breath, I tried to control my emotions. He was doing exactly what I needed him to do without me telling him or guiding him. But the thought of losing him, right after Dylan, hurt my soul.

"You aren't going to lose me," he said, pushing a stray hair behind my ear. "You're stuck with me. Remember?"

"I can't," I muttered.

"I know," he said with a sad smile. "It's fine. You have to admit, I'm pretty damn good."

"I'll never admit that," I said.

"Yes, you will. One day, you will," he said.

Motherfucking, sword-fighting Bard. I fell right for that one.

CHAPTER TEN

WHEN WE ENTERED THE HOUSE, ELLA WAS POURING GLASSES OF sweet tea for everyone. I bowed my head to hide my red face, making my way to the fridge for another orange soda. I wasn't sure what happened to the one I had had outside.

Finley eased over to me, where I was at the kitchen counter. "He really is good. Tennyson said he was shocked, but that he equated it to the work he used to do on the farm back in Texas. He said he's strong and he's learned enough to hold his own in a fight."

"I could see that," I mumbled.

"Then what's the problem? I give him credit for even thinking of it. He's really jumped in to fill roles that Dylan left in town and with you. He coordinates everything with Tennyson for the supplies and needs of the people here. I think you have been so lost in your grief that you haven't noticed," Finley said. "Not that there is anything wrong with that."

"I hadn't noticed," I said as Levi and Astor joked with each other.

"You should. He's not the same lost kid anymore," Finley said. That much I had noticed, but I hadn't realized the depth of it. "You should know that while in Summer, Rhiannon had him brought to her chambers. She tried to force him, but he was able to withstand her."

A low growl crossed my lips, causing everyone in the room to stop talking. I shook my head, waving off their attention.

"He never mentioned it," I said.

"Why should he? Does it matter to you?" Finley asked.

"You're playing a stupid game, Brother," I said.

"It's not stupid if it makes you admit that you do care about him," he said.

"I do care about him. Very much," I said.

"You love him," Finley prodded.

"How are you doing?" I asked changing the subject.

"I'm fine," he replied, taking the hint that I was done with the Levi conversation. I'd already had it once today. I had the feeling that I might have it again in the future. I wasn't fighting the inevitable. I was not in a place where I could make a rational decision about my feelings toward Levi. I was still crying myself to sleep most nights. My heart was clearly broken and torn. I needed more time.

"Really?" I asked.

"Nelly was a mistake. I can't apologize enough. I think with things other than my brain sometimes," Finley replied.

"All men do," I smirked.

"Go ahead and lump us all together, Grace. But that one over there, all he thinks about is you," Finley said with a slight nod to Levi.

"It doesn't really matter right now," I said.

"It will. Someday it will," Finley said. "I've got to get to town. I'm meeting with Mike. He's working on some liquids for me."

"Like?" I asked.

"Stuff that will help in Winter," he said with a grin. "I'll tell you when it works. So far, it hasn't."

"Thanks, Fin," I said.

He kissed me on the cheek. "Love ya, Glory."

I missed my brother. It felt like he was finally back with me. He said his good-byes to Astor, Ella, and Levi. My bard had been very busy and sneaky too. I didn't blame him for not telling me about Rhiannon. There was no way she had persuaded him to do anything with her, especially sex. Otherwise, she would have taunted me with it when we were there. Perhaps Finley was right. I had been so blinded by my own grief even leading up to Dylan's death, that I didn't see all the things that Levi was doing. I didn't want to see him. My focus was on my children. However, I also knew Levi. He wasn't doing it to draw attention to himself.

A vehicle approached from outside. It was Luther bringing Winnie home from her lesson for the day. She was making progress, but she had a long way to go. I was afraid she couldn't understand the power that she had inside of her.

"Want me to go pick up Aydan?" Levi asked.

"If you want," I said.

"Won't take long. I'll be back soon," he said as he hurried out the door. Nestor had picked up Aydan earlier to have a little great granddaddy time with the munchkin while he was still little. As Levi went out the door, Winnie came running in the door barreling into my legs. She held me tightly.

"Hey, honey, what's wrong?" I asked. She just buried her face in my leg. I bent down to look at her in the face. Tears rolled down her cheeks as she shook her head back and forth. Luther appeared at the door with Levi who had stepped back inside.

"She's okay," Luther reassured me.

"What happened?" I asked.

"I hurt something," she said.

"What did you hurt?" I asked.

"An animal," she said.

"It was a roach," Luther said.

"Well, I think that can be forgiven," I said.

"It scared me, and I flamed it!" she exclaimed.

"We were out in my shed looking for some wood to practice her fire on, and the damn thing ran out on her. I probably would have done the same thing. Creepy little shits," Luther said.

"You didn't burn the shed down, did you?" I asked.

"Nah, just a little hole in the wood. She's controlling the spread, just not the knee-jerk reaction," he explained.

"I'm sorry, Momma," she whimpered.

"Winnie, listen to me. Sometimes we make mistakes. It's going to happen. I think if a bug would have jumped out on me I might have frozen it to death! Plus, you need to remember that there are some bugs in this world that need to be squashed. The hard part is learning which bugs to kill and which ones will help you out in the future. It's tough now for you, but we are here with you as you learn. Okay?" I explained.

"Okay, Momma," she said hugging me tightly.

I made eye contact with Levi who had waited behind to see if he was needed. He nodded, then slipped out the door.

"Thank you, Luther, for all of your help with Miss Winnie as she is learning," I said.

"Yes, thank you, Mr. Luther," Winnie said. She rushed across the room, and he bent down to hug her tightly.

"You're welcome, dear child," he said. "Grace, my friend will be here tomorrow. I would like you to meet him as soon as possible."

"Are you going to tell me who or what he is?" I asked.

Luther grinned, "Nope. I want it to be a surprise. Plus, I think there might be a clash of personalities. We will just see."

"You devil," I said. "You want to stay for dinner?"

"No, ma'am. If I don't get back to Betty, she will accuse me of sleeping around on her," he said.

She would probably accuse him of it anyway, but I knew good and well that she didn't mean it, and he loved every minute of it.

"Have a good evening," I said as Astor opened the door to let Luther out.

"So, what's for dinner?" Astor asked.

"I was thinking cheeseburgers," I said.

"Cheeseburgers! Cheeseburgers!" Winnie chanted.

"Burgers it is," Astor said.

"I'll help," I added.

"I'll go play," Winnie said.

"Ella, are you staying for dinner?" I asked.

"Yes, please," she said. "I'll set the table."

～

Just as we sat down to eat, another car approached outside. Levi shifted in his seat, and I knew that suddenly he felt uncomfortable.

"*Who?*" I asked.

"*My father,*" he said rising up to go to the door.

"Invite him to dinner," I said.

Levi grunted, then reached the door as his father knocked. Levi opened the door without saying anything and his father peeked inside.

"Oh, I'm interrupting dinner," he said. "I'll come back later."

"Okay," Levi said.

"Levi! William, why don't you join us? We have plenty," I said.

"I don't want to impose on your family dinner," he said.

I stood up and walked to the door where Levi was trying to control his seethe. "William, you're part of this family. I would like it very much if you would join us more often," I said.

When I looked at him, I realized something different about him. His eyes weren't bloodshot, and he didn't smell like alcohol. He looked very much like Levi sober. Very handsome with deep blue eyes.

"*He's sober,*" Levi said.

"*I see that,*" I replied.

"Are you sure, Grace?" he asked.

"Yes, of course," I said waving him inside. He stepped inside timidly. Astor, Ella, and Winnie smiled at him. Astor stood up, pulling the spare chair to the dining room table.

"Nice to see you, Mr. William," Winnie said. My proper little girl. So proud.

"Good to see you, too, Miss Winnie," he said as he sat down.

"*You okay?*" I asked Levi.

"*I guess,*" he replied. I dared to look. Yep, he was brooding. God bless it.

Dinner went by with a tense, but happy conversation about the upcoming Halloween holiday. I grew up calling it Samhain, but Winnie called it Halloween. We deferred to her young judgment on the matter. We discussed costumes and traditions. She seemed to be very interested in the traditions of honoring the dead. We had already honored Dylan, but it was traditional to do it for the holiday. We were more than happy to allow her to do it again. It was a good coping mechanism not just for her, but for myself as well. William kept quiet most of the night but joined in the conversation occasionally.

After dinner, Levi helped me clear the table while Astor took Ella home.

"Be back soon," he said in a low tone while standing next to Levi and me at the sink.

"I'd rather you not come back," I replied.

"Why? What have I done wrong?" he said.

"Nothing. Yet," I said with a smile.

"Grace," he blushed.

"She's right," Levi said. "Don't come back."

"You two are incorrigible and hypocrites," he smirked, then met his lady at the door.

"Are we hypocrites?" I asked Levi.

Before he could answer, Winnie asked, "What's a hypocrite?"

William who had been sitting in the living room coloring with her laughed at the question. He had a deep rich laugh, and I kinda liked it.

"It's when someone tells you that you should do something, but they don't do it themselves," I said.

"I don't understand," she said.

Levi started giggling. I flicked soapy water at him. He dodged it but kept laughing.

"It's like if you told someone to be kind to a friend, but then you were mean to the friend," William said, helping out with the explanation.

"Oh, okay, it's like a liar," she said, then went back to her coloring. It was enough of an explanation for her. William looked up to Levi, and Levi nodded thanks to him. I had the sudden urge to repair the relationship between father and son, but I had no idea where to start. It seemed that William was trying.

"*Stay out of it, please,*" Levi begged.

"*I just know that I miss my father, and you've never had a good one. You might give him a chance,*" I said.

"*I've given him plenty of chances,*" Levi said. "*He can hang around or do whatever, but I'm not ready to forgive him.*"

I put my hand over his wrist. He shuddered at my touch. "*Don't wait too long to say the things you should.*"

He shook his head, gently pulling away from my grasp. Levi had no connection to William except for blood. I was thankful that William was trying, but it hurt to see him hurting over Levi's rejections. I understood Levi's perspective too. I'd lived many years despising my father. Only to realize lately, that perhaps I was wrong in hating him so intently. It wasn't that I didn't have a reason. I had come to learn that reason wasn't enough when a life drew to a close. There was a bond between a child and their parent that cannot be severed. It could be twisted and torn, but never completely broken. William and Levi had time to mend things. I hoped.

CHAPTER ELEVEN

I spent the morning at the office while Levi ran some errands for Mayor Jenkins. He was much more involved than I had realized. Even the Mayor was leaning on him for things now. Luther would be coming by soon with his ghoul hunter. My plan was to meet this hunter, then pay my dear friend Mable Sanders another visit. I wanted to know who the third ORC was. I believed it important to our survival. The potential for that person to be inside the wards was very high especially since she refused to tell me who it was.

Leaning back in my chair, Aydan sat on my lap clapping his hands and playing with a plastic truck. He moved it back and forth over the desk making raspberries as it moved. He was slobbering everywhere, but it was too cute to stop him from doing it.

A shadow moved outside the window, and I jumped. Aydan sat very still in my lap. I lowered him down behind my desk into the little playpen that I had there. Someone was here.

A dark form drew up out of the floor, then solidified in front of me. The same ghoul from the night at my house stood inside the protected walls of my office. My power was already charged, and I stared at him. Don't mess with a mother.

"Good morning, Queen of the Exiles, I have come to request that you allow us to take what we came here for with a promise to move out of your town with no incidents," he said. His voice drifted out of his blackened body. He looked as if he were a charred piece of wood, brittle and ready to break.

"Get out of my office. You were not invited here," I said.

"I expect no hospitality from you, but I am not afraid of you either," he smiled. The darkness split at his lips revealing red bloody teeth. His eyes flickered for a moment, then Levi stood behind him. "Your bard is powerful."

"Damn straight, I am," Levi growled.

I wasn't going to negotiate with a being that decided to pop into my office unannounced.

"You can make an appointment, and I'll be happy to discuss this with you when I have an opening in my schedule," I said.

He chuckled. "I've heard that you were, how did they put it, sassy."

"I haven't even started sassing you yet," I said.

"You need to leave," Levi said.

"I see. I will not set an appointment. I will just take what I came here for. Just remember, the dead belong to me. You may rule this world and the one under it, but those who have left both are mine."

"Anything living or dead in this town is mine, and I dare you to take it from me," I growled. Aydan responded by stomping in his playpen. A clap of thunder shook the trailer when he did. I tried not to act surprised, but it was very hard.

"Just the same. See you soon," he said slipping back into the floor.

"Good golly, Aydan!" I said spinning around to look at him.

He looked up at me with a grin and clapped his hands together. Levi peered over the desk at him.

"What's worse than having an adolescent with new magical powers?" Levi asked.

"Having an infant with them," I responded.

Within a few moments, the office was filled with my knights, except Luther who called. He said that he and the visitor would be arriving soon.

"I'm fine. We are fine," I said.

"You shouldn't be alone," Astor said.

"I'm a fairy queen," I said.

"Who shouldn't be alone," he countered. Finley stood against the far wall but didn't join the conversation.

"I agree," Tennyson said as he lounged in the other chair in the room besides my own. He leaned back in his fine suit, puffing on a vape mod that was cylindrical making it look like a cigar.

"Get that away from my child," I said.

"Your child just shook the whole town with a clap of thunder. I'm pretty sure this won't hurt him," he said.

"Levi, call Remy. Dylan said something about some of their folk coming to bless him. I don't know what that means, but we should probably look into it," I said. Remington Blake was a star folk of the Native Americans. He had connections all over the United States with the remaining First People. If anyone could help us with Aydan, it would be them.

Levi fished the phone out of his jeans, then stepped into the other room to make the call.

"What did the ghoul want? Was he specific this time?" Troy asked.

"No. Just demanded that I comply," I said.

"And you said?" Tennyson asked.

"I told him he could make an appointment." They all snickered lightly.

"Damn, Grace. You do beat all," Tennyson said. "You've got balls."

"No, she doesn't," Levi said from the other room which caused them to all laugh harder.

"Levi Rearden, I am going to knock you into next week," I said. "I have balls. They are just lady balls."

Astor grunted, and Tennyson continued to laugh.

"I think I'll go check around town and make sure everyone is alright," Troy said. "Keep me updated."

"Will do," I said as he left.

"Remy said he will make some calls, and Tabitha is coming over to check him out," he said.

"I think he's fine," I said. "He was feeding off of me. I've just got to be careful not to provoke him. I think."

"What was this about lady bits?" he asked.

"Not lady bits. Oh, never mind." He had flustered me because when I looked at him, I realized he was just prodding me.

"I do believe she mentioned something about knocking," Tennyson said adding to the tease.

"Seriously, a ghoul came past all of our protections, into this room with my child, and you guys are too busy trying to get me off-kilter."

"It's working," Levi grinned.

I huffed a long sigh and leaned back into my chair.

"Grace, I believe that he couldn't have harmed you had he tried. He crossed the wards without permission. I'm willing to bet he had no power. You probably could have destroyed him," Tennyson said.

"I felt him outside before he came in," I said.

"And inside?" Levi asked.

"I dunno. I was too busy being momma bear," I said.

"The wards are stronger at home. You need to stay there," Levi said. "And I'll make arrangements to be with you."

"You have taken on responsibilities," I said.

Tennyson cut his eyes to Levi, and Levi winced. "Finley told you," he said.

"Yes," I replied.

"I wasn't hiding it from you," he said in his defense.

"I'm not angry, Levi. I'm proud of you. I'm thankful for you," I said. Then I pointed a finger at Tennyson, "However, you're encouraging him. Tread lightly, Knight."

"He needs very little encouragement, Grace. Just support," he said. "I knew a man just like him once."

"Don't say it," I said.

"I won't, but the similarities are uncanny," he said. "Your father even had a knack for music. Do you remember?"

"I remember," Astor added.

I thought back to my childhood, and I did remember my father playing the lute as well as other instruments. Taliesin had taught him how to play some of them on their long journeys. It was something to do as they traveled. He had nowhere near the musical talent that Levi had, but I didn't think that Tennyson was sold on Levi's music. He saw Levi as a potential leader.

"If I promise to stay at home with the kids other than to go out with one of you, will you continue your duties?" I asked Levi.

He questioned my intentions, but he answered with his heart. "I would like to continue what I'm doing for the town. You know that if there is trouble, I can be with you in an instant."

"Very well. No more office hours until the ghoul problem is solved," I said.

"Thank you, Grace," Levi said.

"You're welcome, Dublin," I replied. Tennyson seemed quite happy with the situation. He stood up straightened his coat and retrieved his sword from beside the chair where he had leaned it against the wall.

"I would like to know things when the two of you are up to something. No more surprise sword fights," I said.

Tennyson nodded. "He is very good. The best I've ever taught, but as you wish, we will keep you informed. We weren't slighting you, my Queen. We were just giving you room to grieve. We are here to back you up and cover the holes that you cannot."

"Thank you, Tennyson," I said.

"Finley, come with me. I have a task for you," he said. Finley pushed himself off the wall.

"For the record, I think you can handle yourself," he said with a smile.

"Sucking up won't get you anywhere, Finley," Tennyson scolded.

"I got your back," Finley grinned. He didn't mean it. He was just disagreeing with them to disagree. He thought I shouldn't be alone here without protection, too. He followed Tennyson out the door who left in a cloud of vape smoke. Levi picked Aydan up from the crib and sat in the chair that Tennyson vacated. He bounced Aydan on his knee. The little man giggled and clapped.

"Astor, I told you not to come home last night," I said turning to the ginger.

"Um, I've got something I need to go do. Call me if you need me," he said as he hurried out the door.

"Trouble in paradise?" I asked.

"More like he's frustrated, and you aren't helping," Levi scolded.

"Perhaps," I said.

"Mayor Jenkins has asked me to take over his job," Levi announced suddenly.

"What?"

"You said you wanted to know everything. I'm telling you," he said. "I've never lied to you, Grace. I won't start now, but I have been working toward forming relationships just in case he really decides that I become the mayor here. The guardian of the Vale."

"This shit just gets deeper and deeper," I said.

"Aydan, it's a good thing you can't talk, because your mommy would teach you all sorts of bad words," Levi said.

"Sorry." Levi just laughed. "Mayor?"

"Yes," he said.

"Isn't there supposed to be an election for that? We aren't having any more elections in this town," I said. The last one was a disaster which resulted in my father's death.

"No, he's not really mayor. He's the protector of the Vale, and he said since I had warded it with the spell from the book that maybe I would be the best candidate to keep it protected. I can feel everything that moves in an out of it from the smallest rabbit to the biggest troll. It only makes sense," he said.

"To be honest, I want the Vale and what it stands for destroyed," I said.

"What?"

"I don't want to destroy Shady Grove. I want to destroy the curse so that the people here can live, die, and return as was intended for our kind. Not to be cursed into an oblivion," I said thinking about Dylan.

"Your father's spirit rejoined the tree. I would think that anyone that died here would continue on in that manner," Levi said. "Perhaps even Dylan could talk to you at the stone if Lilith would allow it."

The thought had crossed my mind, but my stone and circle drew power from the tree and the Otherworld. Lilith said that Dylan was there in peace. I wouldn't want to disturb that. Not after all he had been through. It didn't matter how hard it hurt. It would be selfish for me to want him to return that way.

"No," I said.

"I was just trying to give you hope," Levi said. "Sometimes you drift too far away."

"I'm here. My hope is in my children," I said.

"Good," he said.

"And you," I added.

"*Thank you, my Queen,*" he said as he continued to bounce Aydan on his knee.

CHAPTER TWELVE

"Whatever you've got here, I will kill," he paused and narrowed his eyes. "For the right price."

"I doubt payment will be an obstacle," I replied.

Rostam Dastan, Luther's supernatural hunter, was none other than the Persian equivalent to Greece's Achilles. They both had girly hair and egos the size of an elephant. I wasn't sure what Dastan's weakness was, but I was sure I could find out if needed. We would start with the ankle and work our way up. His first name was Farrokhzad which meant "Made by God." He was basically a demigod. And from the first moment that I saw him, I hated him.

He lounged back in the chair that he made Levi vacate when he entered the room smoking a real cigar. Levi had to take Aydan outside. Luther remained in the room as I talked to the asshole.

"Honey, I'm a high-priced whore. Perhaps an heir to the Winter throne," he said.

"You may leave," I said.

He sat there staring at me as if I were joking. I moved papers around on my desk, then pulled a pen out of my drawer to start looking over them. They were just documents that Levi had, showing all the supplies and needs of the community. I had no intention of writing on them, but it was a good show.

He laughed while stroking his long black beard; his dark eyes watched my movements. "You intend to dismiss me after my long journey? I came here to kill. You're very disrespectful for one so young," he said.

The tattoo on my arm flared. I was already walking around as a blonde on a daily basis, but I kept the power concealed. It rushed over my skin revealing the intricate skin markings surging with Winter power. I slowly stood to my feet as the room turned to ice including the chair that the prick sat on.

"Do not assume by my appearance that I am young, Rostam Datsan. I've handled many beasts in my day. You would be the least of them," I said as the trailer shook with power. Levi stood at the door with Aydan strapped to his back in a carrier. His tattoo fed off my power. The strings of the guitar glowed waiting to be played.

I stalked toward the man as he wrapped his fingers around the hilt of his sword. Maybe Levi having a sword wasn't a bad idea.

"Prince Dastan, perhaps we can come to a mutual understanding. You don't have to like each other to work together," Luther offered.

"Unsheathe that blade. Let's see what you can do," I said, looming over him.

"*Easy, Grace,*" Levi said.

"*I'm going to easy him right out the door,*" I responded.

"I do not wish to cause you harm, honored Queen. Forgive my rudeness," he said releasing the hilt. I backed away from him to lean on the desk. At that point, I realized that my clothes had changed to the long black dress I wore the night my father returned to the tree. The scrolls of skin art continued to roll with Winter power as I stared at him.

"If you decide to work for me, one thing that is required is respect. If you don't freely give it, I will make you earn it, but you won't like that," I said.

The Prince didn't like to be told what to do, but for whatever reason, he decided to stay in Shady Grove and work to remove the ghouls.

"It would be an honor to be in your employ," he said, bowing his head. Levi stepped back into the other room, releasing the power that he held.

"Good. Let's talk payment," I said.

"My favorite part," he replied.

After negotiating overpayment, we came to an understanding. I would have to make a few calls to retrieve the items he wanted, but I was sure that I could obtain the things he had requested. They seemed like odd requests, but I was sure I could handle it.

"Now, who are the ghouls after?" he asked.

"They haven't said," I replied.

"Someone in your town is hiding something from you," Dastan replied.

"I'm sure there are more than one. I don't need or want to know the private lives of my people. As long as there is no trouble. And when there is, the troublemaker usually reveals themselves," I said.

"Old friend, surely you know who they are after. It would be one of our own people," Dastan said. I looked to Luther who had the same look as he did in my home after the ghouls first appeared.

"Luther, who are they after?" I asked.

He put his hands on his hips and heaved a heavy sigh. "Betty. They are after Betty," he said. "But they can't have her. And I will pay Dastan's fee if necessary."

"No, she is under my protection, but they came for the dead," I said.

"She is Banshee," Luther said.

"Madar Sag," Dastan muttered.

"You're married to an ancestral spirit? How is that possible?" I asked.

"You're a fairy queen in a trailer park. You tell me," Luther said becoming agitated.

"Luther, if she is Banshee, then she has a job to do on this earth, why would the ghouls want to take her?" I asked.

"She no longer does her duties," he said. "She still knows who will die. She knew that Dylan would. It took everything she had not to sing the lament for him, but she kept quiet. No one knows what she is. It's easier that they don't."

"I've only ever gotten Unseelie Fairy from her," I replied.

"She conceals it," Luther said. "It's a very good spell."

"Apparently," I said. "This is neither here nor there. I'm not willing to part with her for any damn ghoul. Perhaps we don't need Prince Dastan."

"Wait a minute, now. I came here to capture ghouls. It's what I do," he said.

"You're here for a paycheck. You will be paid for your time either way," I replied.

"Why don't we need him?"

"If we negotiate with the ghouls, then perhaps they will move on," I said.

"Diplomacy? Really, Grace? Not your style," Luther said.

"At least one thing I can admire in her," Dastan remarked.

"Quiet before I start testing out my theory on you," I said.

"You're more than welcome to test whatever you would like," Dastan said.

"Bugger off," I replied. He chuckled, then took a deep draw on his cigar. "Maybe if Betty would agree to resume her duties, then they would move on."

"She doesn't want to do that," Luther said. "But I'm not sure that will deter them."

"We can try. I'll talk to her," I said. "Hold your horses, Prince. Let me see if we can avoid conflict."

"Fine. Point me to the closest establishment serving liquor," Dastan said.

"Luther, do you mind?" I asked.

"I'll take him to Hot Tin. Then I need to tell Betty that I told you. If you don't see me again, I want you to know I thank you for standing up for her," he said.

"She isn't going to hurt you, Luther. That woman loves you," I said.

"Yes, but Grace remember when you realized everyone knew your secret. You weren't happy about it. She won't be either," he said.

"Levi and I will come see her tonight," I said. "We will talk about it."

"Alright," he conceded.

I walked the men to the door, watching Luther slump his shoulders. No wonder they had the weird exchange at my house. Betty was basically a fairy spirit. She had a damn good spell. I'd like to know who set it up for her because I would have never guessed.

"How do you fall in love with a ghost?" Levi asked.

"I dunno. Ask Demi Moore," I replied.

"Aston Kutcher isn't dead," Levi replied.

I laughed. "No, have you never seen the movie Ghost?" I asked.

"Guess not," he replied. He was sitting on the couch with Aydan asleep on his chest.

"She was in love with a ghost," I replied. "It was endearing but weird."

"That about sums it up," he said. "Very weird."

"You can't treat her differently," I said.

"I won't. I love Betty. She's awesome," he said. "We will figure it out."

Dylan would know what to do. He was always good at these kinds of things. He was able to get people to trust him. He would know exactly what to say to put Betty at ease. There was no doubt that I would protect her as I was sworn to do. Betty was family. Ghouls or not, she was staying in Shady Grove where she belonged.

I couldn't imagine what it was like for her to know that deaths were coming. She must have known every life I've taken. I wondered how it worked. Did she have dreams or visions? Was it an instinct? I hoped she would open up to me about it. I crossed the room, joining Levi and Aydan on the couch. Watching my son sleep, I was reminded of how much he looked like his father. Although Aydan's hair had developed an interesting curl to it when it was long. It was still the sandy brown just like his father's hair. Levi watched me as I gently brushed Aydan's hair as he slept.

Tears threatened to slide down my cheeks, but I pushed them back. Instead, I leaned over on Levi, resting my head on his shoulder. We sat there together until Aydan stirred, then we went home to prepare for a visit with a banshee.

CHAPTER THIRTEEN

Astor and Ella volunteered to watch the kids while Levi and I went to see Betty and Luther at their home. They decided to close up the diner for the night. They did that more often these days as the population in Shady Grove had dropped when the humans left. When Betty called me to invite me to her home, I knew she wasn't happy. I just hoped that we could reach a reasonable conclusion to avoid any more ghoul activity. I wasn't sure how they were going to eat a spirit woman, but perhaps when they consumed the body, they also consumed the soul. I hoped to learn a lot more about it this evening.

"You're nervous," Levi said as he drove the truck.

"I am. Betty is my friend, and I don't want the ghouls to take her. Luther is right. I know exactly what it feels like when your secret is exposed," I said.

"They already accepted you for who you were," he said.

"That is the difference," I said. "But I'm sure the pain is similar."

"Pain?"

"I felt betrayed. Everyone for years moved around me like I was a normal human, but all the while they knew who and what I was," I said.

"They were living the lie that Jeremiah constructed," he said.

"Fucking Jeremiah," I said.

"Yeah, his name should have been Carl," Levi said.

"Huh?" I asked.

"Just something I read in a book," he said.

"Oh, okay," I said dismissing it.

We pulled into the driveway of a lovely, full-brick home. The roof pitched high with three dormer windows across the front. A whitewashed porch stretched half the length of the house. The landscaping was pristine and well kept. A glow from the windows of the house made it feel like a home.

I didn't know Luther and Betty's story, but I wished they would tell it to me. I knew that it involved the deaths of both of their spouses. I wondered if that had something to do with why Betty abandoned her Banshee duties or perhaps how she became a Banshee in the first place.

We approached the front door, and Levi knocked politely.

Betty opened the door wearing a dress straight out of a 1950's Sears catalog. She wiped her hands on an apron and smiled at us through bright red lipstick.

"Welcome, Grace and Levi. Please come in. I was just finishing up the dishes. Can I get you something to drink or a bite to eat?" she asked using proper Southern and Fairy Hospitality. We entered the home and took seats in the living room. The house was surprisingly quiet. I wanted to ask about Luther, but I didn't. "Let me just put up this apron, and I'll be right back."

"*Where is Luther? Can you feel him?*" Levi asked. Luther felt a little like Dylan with his warmth, but darker. At the moment, I didn't feel anything like that. The house was protected though. We weren't in any danger from Betty due to hospitality.

"*No. I barely feel you. Like there is a spell here,*" I said.

"*Could she be the third ORC?*" Levi asked.

It would be a devastating proposition. It would make my assumptions wrong about Mable and Robin. Betty would out age them both making her the crone. It couldn't be, and I refused to consider it.

"*No*," I responded. Levi pursed his lips, then shook his head. He knew I was refusing to believe anything bad about my friend.

"There. Now I'm presentable," Betty said with a huge smile. "I declare, Levi, you get more handsome every time I see you."

"Thank you, Betty," he said.

"Gene tells me that you might become Shady Grove's Mayor. Is that true?" she asked.

"It is. We are working for a solution," Levi admitted.

"Wonderful. You have really stepped up, and I appreciate it as well as the council and the fairies here. You're one of us, Levi," she said. The whole conversation felt tense and rehearsed.

"I'm going to do my best," Levi said looking at me.

"You're going to let him do it, right?" she asked me.

"I wouldn't stand in his way," I responded.

"I'm surprised. You seem to like to control everything," Betty said.

"I'm not the same woman I used to be, plus Levi is his own man. He decides what he wants to do, and whatever he decides I support," I said.

"You have changed a lot over the past year, Grace," she said. "There was a time that I had my doubts about you, but you've pulled through. I hoped that Dylan's death wouldn't impede your progress."

"If anything, Dylan's death has given me a reason to complete what I set out to do," I said. "He believed in me from the beginning."

"I'm glad you remember that now. It was rough on him," she said. "I'm sorry. You didn't come here to talk about such sad subjects. Luther says you have a proposal for me regarding the ghouls."

"Yes. It is my theory that they are after you because you no longer keen, wail, or lament. It's possible that now to them, you're just a dead soul to be consumed. If you would consider continuing your Banshee duties, then maybe they would move on."

"No," she said flatly.

"I would like to end this diplomatically with them if we could. We have much bigger fights," I said.

"Just give me to them," she said.

"Absolutely not," I replied. "You're under my protection, and if we have to fight them, then we will."

"Then what? Every Samhain they will return to claim me," she said.

"Then we will fight them every fucking year," I said.

She lowered her head to look at the flowery rug on the floor. "I don't deserve to be protected like that."

"Betty Stallworth, you were one of my first friends here. At first, I thought you were just playing the sweet waitress role to get tips, but you've turned out to be a great friend. I know we haven't always seen eye to eye on things, but that isn't necessary. When it gets down to the nitty gritty, I've got your back," I said.

"So, do I," Levi echoed the sentiment.

"How am I supposed to keen for the coming dead in this town? The curse makes death something we fear. We were all sent here because of our past actions," she said.

"I want to erase that curse. It means more to me than taking back Winter," I said.

"What?"

"I have every intention of finding a way to break the vale. The fairies here deserve a second chance just like everyone else," I said.

"Some of us have done very bad things," she said.

"But none of them do it now. Except for maybe Mable and Stephanie," I said.

"Haven't heard her name in a while," she muttered.

"No, she's a prisoner to Brockton like Dylan and Levi were," I said.

"Will you rescue her?" Betty asked.

"No," I replied. "Not for the grief that she caused me, but for the hell she put Dylan through. For how she used Joey Blankenship. For abandoning her child."

"Spoken like a true mother," she said. "I would have never

guessed you would become a mother. A wonderful mother."

"I must have been horrible when I came here," I said.

"No, you were polite and kind. Sassy, but in a good way. But you didn't seem like mother material," she said.

"She's still all of that," Levi smirked.

I swatted at him, and he jumped to the other end of the couch. Betty finally grinned watching us.

"She's already threatened to knock me into next week," Levi whined.

"Oh, you poor thing. Aunt Betty can make it better," she said with a wink. Levi blushed.

I quickly looked back to Betty who saw me avoiding the attraction between us.

"Damn he's adorable when he blushes," she said.

"Please stop," Levi begged.

"Yes, he is, if I didn't want to jerk a wart on him," I said.

"What happened to jerking a knot in my tail?" he asked.

"You equate that with swapping gravy, so I'm changing it. If you find a way to make sex and warts the same thing, I'm disowning you," I said.

"You don't own me anyway," he sassed.

"Just makes it easier to get rid of you," I said.

"You would never," Betty scolded.

Levi opened his mouth to speak, but I beat him to it.

"Never," I responded. Levi's jaws clamped shut. He had nothing more to say, but Betty died laughing. "It's good to hear you laugh. Now I'm going to dare to ask the question."

"Where is Luther?" she said for me.

"Yeah," I said.

She crossed the room opening a curio cabinet. She pulled out a tall bottle with a capped lid. The bulb at the bottom was covered in hand-painted swirls. The deep crimson color of the bottle was accented by gold, white, and orange jewels.

"Dear God," I said.

She uncorked the lid. A dark billowing smoke boiled out of the bottle forming the shape of a man, then it solidified into Luther, the

Ifrit. He had told me he was a cursed Marid. I didn't imagine he had a bottle, but apparently, he did. His Banshee wife owned him.

"Thank you, my Love," he said, bending over to kiss her red lips. She turned her head from him, so he planted the kiss on her cheek. "Good evening, Grace. Levi."

"Hello, Luther," I said. "Nice bottle."

"It's cramped," he said with a smile.

"Stop complaining. That's what you get for telling my secret. My secret! The one I should have been given the opportunity to tell," she yelled at him.

"*I'd rather sleep in the doghouse than that thing,*" he said.

"*You keep it up, and Rufus will have a roommate,*" I said.

"*Whatever. You love arguing with me,*" he smirked.

I decided not to comment on the truth of his statement.

"You're right," Luther agreed.

"What am I going to do with you?" she asked him.

"Whatever you want," he said.

"Not in front of the children," she grinned.

"No, go right ahead," I said, smiling at them both.

"Won't you consider her offer?" Luther asked.

"You sit down and hush," Betty scolded him.

"Yes, ma'am," he replied. He sat across from us on a loveseat with a huge grin on his face. I wasn't sure why he was so happy, but he was. I imagined if my love had the ability to stuff me in a bottle, I'd be happy to be out in whatever circumstances.

"*I'm going to get you a bottle,*" Levi said.

Instead of entertaining his juvenile notion, I turned back to the *important* conversation in the room. "I don't have to know the story, but is there a reason why you won't return to your duties as Banshee?"

"Yes, and it's a very good reason. Plus, did you want me to wail for Dylan before he died?" she asked.

"Why not? I did," I said. "There were times when I knew inside of me that he wasn't coming back. Every pore on my body wailed."

"People will want to know," she said.

"I don't have to know for myself. As far as that goes, I can order everyone not to ask you," I said.

"My family are the people of Shady Grove. I feel their deaths before they come. It aches me to the core, but then not to be able to release it. To put on a happy face and go to the diner. It's been awful," she said.

"Then it's time to be yourself. None of us will ever think less of you," I said. "Or Luther."

"She's right. We love you, Betty," Levi said.

"Oh, Darlin', I love you too," she said.

Darlin'.

I sighed, but only Levi noticed. He inched closer to me on the couch.

"Can I have a little time to think about it?" Betty asked. Luther threaded his fingers through hers.

"Of course," I replied.

"Thank you for coming by," Betty said.

The moment we hit the truck, Levi started talking.

"She didn't realize she said it," he said.

"I know," I replied.

"I know I'm not him, and you know it. That's all that matters," he said.

"It's not all that matters, but in this case, yeah," I said staring into the darkness. It seemed abnormally dark. I allowed myself to sink into it as we drove the rest of the way home. When we arrived, the kids were already in bed. I excused myself after thanking Astor and Ella for keeping them. Levi didn't say anything else to me. I felt his presence there, but he didn't speak. Which was exactly what I needed.

After fighting it for so long, I went to the closet. The smell of mint and leather drifted around me when I opened the door. I took the jacket off the hanger, then curled up in the bed with it. It was empty and was missing the warmth of him. However, I needed the comfort of the memory of him. Our memories.

CHAPTER FOURTEEN

LEVI

"HELLO," I GRUMBLED INTO THE PHONE.

"Levi, we need to talk," Riley said.

"What time is it?" I asked.

"2 a.m.," she replied.

"I can't leave the house. The kids are here," I said.

"Is their mother there?" she asked.

"What the hell do you want, Riley?" I asked.

"Just skip to me. Just for a minute," she begged.

"No," I said, hanging up the phone.

Before I could lay it on the nightstand, it rang again. I turned the ringer off and sent it to voicemail. It continued to ring. Even though it was on silent and turned over, I knew it was ringing. I got up and walked into the darkened hallway. I looked down at Grace's room. I got a faint whiff of leather. I knew what that meant. She was in a place that I couldn't help or shouldn't. More like she didn't want me to help. Some of this she had to work through on her own.

"Silence," I said as the strings of my guitar tattoo let out a silent wave of music. My footsteps drowned in the spell, and I walked through the house like a ghost.

I reached the fridge, then I took out a can of coke. Even the snap of the can's lid was silent. Taking long draws of the drink, I felt the harsh cold flow down my throat. It felt good. There was a light tap on the back door. I froze to make sure I wasn't hearing anything.

Tap. Tap.

"Fuck," I muttered. Well, I tried to mutter, but it was silenced. "Dispel."

The silence spell wilted, and I stepped lightly to the back door. When I opened it, Riley stepped inside.

"Get the fuck out of this house," I growled at her.

"No, you listen to me. You hate me all you want, but there is something you need to know. The third ORC is not in Shady Grove," she said.

"How do you know that?" I asked.

"Robin is from Summer. I talked to some people from Summer, and Robin mentioned that she was training someone to be her heir. She's not bothered to bring a child into the world," she said.

"Thank the gods," I said.

"Right? Well, I'm still trying to find out who it is, but I don't know yet," she said.

"This could have waited until morning or you could have told me on the phone," I said.

"Well, I had hoped to see you half-naked," she said reaching for me in the darkness.

I backed away from her holding my hand out to stop her advance. "Riley, get out," I said. "Please."

"You remember us, right?" she said.

"I do. I remember being collared," I said.

"You weren't collared on Valentine's when you played your guitar for me," she purred. "You could play your new one for me. I'd love it. You could do whatever you wanted to me. It would just be sex, Levi. Really, good sex."

"No, Riley, get off me," I said shoving her away. I backed into the living room.

"Shh! She will hear you," Riley said.

"She already does," I said.

A light blue glow floated across the upstairs banister, then down the steps one by one. She was wearing a long white nightgown and a leather jacket. The glow of her skin markings showed through the sheer gown. I gulped watching her move slowly down the steps. Riley backed up into the kitchen.

"Stop," Grace muttered. Time stood still, except for me. I could feel the panic rising up inside of Riley.

She stalked slowly over to where Riley stood in between the kitchen and the living room. I wanted to speak, but I didn't know what to say. Grace knew I was trying to get her out of the house. She also knew I let her in the house.

"You're so beautiful, Riley. You could have any man in this town you wanted, except for the one that doesn't want you. Yet you continue on. How am I supposed to have faith in your information if you break the laws of hospitality? I could put you down right now. You know that, right?" Grace asked as she floated around Riley. "Oh, that's right. You can't speak. It's no nevermind because I'm not going to kill you. You will continue to get information, but instead of bringing it to Levi, you will report to me. Is that clear?"

Riley blinked, then the time spell let go. "You can't make me," she gasped.

"It is the task I assign you instead of killing you for coming into my home with my children, uninvited," Grace stated.

"As you wish," Riley said.

"Hmm," Grace pondered, then moved close to Riley's ear and whispered something.

Riley closed her eyes tightly. "As you wish, my Queen."

"Wonderful. Now get out," Grace said. The order shook the house. Riley turned on her heel and sprinted to the back door. She fumbled with the knob but ran into the night without shutting the door.

Grace lowered to the floor releasing the power. The blue glow faded as she shut the back door waving her hand on it to restore the ward that was broken when Riley came in.

I braced myself for her wrath, but instead, she turned around to me a broken woman. Just a beautiful woman in a nightgown and the jacket of her dead fiancé. She already knew that Riley forced her way in the door. I had nothing to explain. Her bare feet padded across the floor to me. Her cool fingers traced the scar on my face.

"I hope I didn't wake the kids," she whispered.

"We would have heard them by now if you had," I said.

She leaned in and kissed me on the cheek. "Get to bed, Levi," she said.

"I will as soon as I finish this," I said holding up the coke.

"Okay," she muttered, then slowly walked back up the stairs. Her pace was more of a trudge than the gentle floating way she had descended them earlier. I looked up to watch her walk out of sight. She didn't look back.

I wanted to comfort her, but she did not want to be comforted. She wanted to feel the pain and loss. I just wanted to see her happy again. A deep rich happiness that had left her with his death. Everything felt so empty with her now. Her happiness on the surface didn't reach her heart.

The heart that mine desired. I wanted to be the one to make her feel again. Grace's heart had always made her different from the other fairies. She feared now that she would become just like the darkest of them. This display with Riley was just a ghost of her power. Her heart kept her in check. Since she didn't evaporate Riley on the spot, I had to think she still had that heart. I knew that she did. I shouldn't question it, but as each day passed, I felt like she was slipping further away from me.

Beyond anything that happened in the Otherworld, I'll never forget what Dylan told me in one of his sane moments.

"Levi, she will be a pain in the ass. She won't want to give in. You know how she is. Just hang in there, and in the end, she will be yours."

I was hanging the best I knew how, but the end seemed a long way off.

I finished off the coke and decided that I had pondered on this for too long. One of us had to stay positive.

When I reached my bed, my phone continued to blink. I erased the voice messages that Riley left, but she had texted me as well.

RILEY: *I would do anything to get you back.*

I deleted it and went to sleep.

CHAPTER FIFTEEN

GRACE

THE DOOR CLOSED ONCE AGAIN ON THE LEATHER JACKET. THAT relapse might have cost Riley's life. I don't know what she thought she was doing in my house that late at night, but she clearly had lost her mind. Information or not, I should have known that she would try to go after Levi again. She had remained quiet. However, Levi was resolute. His hatred for her never wavered as she pawed at him.

I told myself I wasn't jealous. A fairy queen had issues telling lies, but apparently, I was fine at telling them to myself.

As I went to bed, I felt Levi fighting his urge to comfort me. Even that was a comfort. He was trying very hard to do the right thing by me and by Dylan. My problem was, I wasn't sure what the right thing was. For him, he had decided to wait for me. It wasn't a move I intended to make. He might be waiting for a very long time.

I turned my focus to the town. I wanted to talk to Nestor to see if he would be willing to confront Mable. He hadn't wanted anything to do with her, but I think she really did love him. Her love just conflicted with her agenda to destroy me. If she wanted to destroy me, then she could have taken Nestor out.

Suddenly, I remembered the fire at Hot Tin Roof after my trial. Nestor was hurt badly in that fire. Surely that witch didn't set Hot Tin on fire with my grandfather in it! The moment she admitted to it, I was going to rip her throat out.

There was a knock on the door that broke me out of my fury.

"Grace," Levi called out to me. I looked down and my hands were balled up into fists. My nails were digging into my skin. I released the anger, then flexed my fingers.

"Come in," I muttered.

He stepped inside with a worried look on his face. "You okay?"

"Remember the fire at Hot Tin?" I asked.

"Of course, we were in the kitchen at the trailer when you saw the smoke," he said.

"Mable," I said.

"No. You think?" he asked.

"Yeah," I said. "I'm going to talk to Nestor. Could you get Winnie ready for school, and watch Ayden until Astor gets here?"

"Astor isn't here?" he asked.

"No," I said, then a smile crossed my face.

"You don't think…"

"Maybe. If not, they are one step closer," I said.

"You would get excited about someone else swapping gravy," he said.

"I am excited for Astor because he is a good man. He deserves to get laid," I said.

"I'm a good man," Levi said.

"No, you aren't," I said. "I've seen inside your head."

"Grace!" he exclaimed.

"What? You've seen inside mine, too," I said.

"Yeah," he said. "But I wasn't trying."

"Whatever, Bard," I taunted him. "I'm going to town."

"Someone is supposed to be with you," he said.

As I walked past him, I popped him on the butt. "You're with me," I said.

Just as my foot hit the top step, he said, "Not like I wanna be."

"I heard that," I called up to him.

"*Good,*" he said.

It made me smile, and I didn't do much of that lately.

Driving to town, I passed the spot where Dylan and I found the older man who had wandered off from his caretaker. It was the same day that we slept together. I remembered that day much differently now knowing his perspective on things. Before he was taken, he and I had a picnic there. I turned the truck around. First, it was the leather jacket. Now it was the picnic spot. I might as well get it out of my system.

I climbed out of the truck and pulled my leather jacket which he bought for me closed. A cool wind blew. The clouds covered the sun. Reaching out with my senses, I knew I only had a few minutes before it started to rain. Walking up to the creek, I watched the water rush by in a torrent. We had had some rain over the last few days. Not that I had noticed. The creek jumped over rocks and carried debris from the forest with it. Pinecones, sticks, and leaves.

The leaves were changing colors. I looked up into the surrounding trees and watched the leaves cascade down around me. The trees were weeping. I walked over to touch a nearby oak.

It spoke to me of my own sadness. I explained to it the death of my mate. The tree shook, shedding more leaves for me. Leaning forward, I kissed the trunk of it.

"Bless you. You honor me," I said.

When speaking to trees, I get images and impressions, but this tree spoke very clearly, "My Queen."

Even the trees were counting on me. No more leather jackets and no more creek side visits. I had a war to fight.

CHAPTER SIXTEEN

ENTERING THE NEARLY EMPTY BAR, I WALKED TOWARD NESTOR WHO plopped a cup on the counter knowing exactly what I needed. Pouring the dark roasted goodness in my cup, I watched the glittering spell shimmer in the liquid. Just the sight of it was as calming as the coffee. I took the seat next to a young man whom I hadn't met before.

He had dark hair which had to be almost black, but it was hard to tell exactly in the dim lighting of the Hot Tin Roof Bar. His jawline had a bladed edge that led down to a square chin and large lips. Big kissable ones. When he tilted his head up from the clear liquid in his glass, his eyes flickered yellow then back to brown.

"Werewolf," I said.

"My Queen, it is a pleasure to formally meet you. I'm Dominick Meyer," he said offering me his hand.

"Ah, yes, it is nice to meet you," I said, shaking his hand.

"I hear the coffee is good here," he said starting up small talk.

"It is, but the liquor is better," I smiled.

He laughed, "It *is* good when you need a little." He picked up his glass and finished off the little bit he had left. Nestor reached to refill it, but Dominick put his hand over the glass refusing another.

"You done?" I asked.

"Yeah. I just got off my shift and wanted to wind down a little. I should probably get home," he said.

"Oh! Do you have a family?" I asked.

"No, maybe someday, but not right now," he said.

"How did you hear about Shady Grove? Why did you come here?" I asked while sipping on my coffee. I was feeling better already, but Dominick winced at my questions. "I'm sorry. Just making small talk. I'm not asking in any kind of official capacity."

"Well, there were rumors of a town where a fairy queen was taking in exiles, and since I was kicked out of my pack, I decided to give it a try. I'm glad I'm here. The scenery is beautiful," he said as his eyes met mine.

My heart thumped hard once. It had been a long time since someone had paid a compliment to me like that. It was corny, but I tended to like that kind of thing. It was honest and a sweet approach. Added to that was the fact that Dominick was someone new. It wasn't my old friends telling me what they thought. It was a virile man.

"I'm sorry, Grace. I mean, my Queen. I didn't mean anything by it. I mean, you're a rare beauty, but I know about your recent loss, and I wouldn't presume to...ah, shit, I'm sorry," he sputtered.

"Please," I said, putting my hand over his. I could feel the warm animal inside of him. I'd been with a shifter or two in my day, but never a wolf. It was almost as though I could feel the feral desire inside that he was holding back. Dominick may have come off as an unassuming flirt, but inside of him, he carried a beast that craved carnal contact. I knew that kind of internal battle. I had waged it from the moment I moved to Shady Grove up until I was with Dylan. Then he was all I wanted. "It's alright. I know you didn't mean anything by it."

He looked down at my hand covering his and shivered. "Your hands are cold," he said.

"Comes with the territory. Thank you for the compliment," I said, trying to reassure him. His heart was pounding in his chest, and I could feel his urge to run from the bar. He'd stepped in a pile of shit and it was too late to scrape it off his shoes.

"Grace," Levi's voice came from the direction of the door. I hadn't felt his presence, but I had been locking my grief away. Not just from myself, but from him too. Earlier when I had made the stop at the creek, I knew I had shut him out enough to keep him away.

"Hey, Dublin, come meet Dominick Meyer," I said as I removed my hand from the wolf's. Levi hadn't taken his eyes off the physical contact since I noticed him there behind us.

"We've met," Levi said slowly walking toward us.

Dominick stumbled off the stool and offered his hand to shake Levi's, "Good to see you, Mr. Rearden."

Levi shook his hand while locking eyes with him.

"*Cool it,*" I demanded.

"*I'm cool,*" he said.

"*You look like you're about to beat his face in,*" I said.

"*I am,*" Levi replied.

"*Dublin! I mean it,*" I hissed. "Nestor, please get Levi a cup of coffee."

"Sure thing," he said promptly pouring a cup then setting it down on the opposite side of me from the wolf.

"Well, I see you have important stuff to talk about. It was a pleasure meeting you, Grace," Dominick stammered under Levi's unyielding gaze.

"*Stop it. Now!*" I demanded. Levi growled at the command but had no choice but to back off.

"It was nice meeting you, too," I replied. "*What has gotten into you?*"

"*He should have some respect,*" Levi said.

"*Goddess bless it, Levi. I was having a conversation with him. That's all. I touched him, so it wasn't like he was pawing me. There is a giant Phoenix-sized hole still in my heart. I ache with his loss, but one thing is for sure, my mind is not absent.*"

Levi looked up to me with regret and an ounce of confusion in his eyes. I swiveled around on the stool just as Dominick made it to the door.

"Oh, Dominick," I said, watching his eyes bug out of his head as I crossed my legs. I knew how to play this game far too well.

"Um, yea?" he said swallowing.

"Does Troy know you're an Alpha too?" I asked.

"*Fuck*," Levi muttered catching on to my game.

When I touched him, he felt different than the other wolves, except Troy. That magical whatsit that made him Alpha surged under his skin. I had suspected, but touching him sealed the deal. The color ran from his face as Levi turned to look back at him.

"I haven't mentioned it," he said.

I slid off the barstool stalking towards him. Overt sexuality is power, especially when you've caught someone in a lie. Someone that has an animal scratching to get out. The one inside of me tended to do cartwheels instead. Had I not been grieving my fiancé and keeping my bard at arm's length, she probably would have done a round-off backhand spring with a twist for the handsome, displaced Alpha wolf.

"So, my question is, are you here to cause trouble or are you going to tell Troy and swear your allegiance to the local Alpha?" I asked as I stopped right in front of him.

"Forgive me. I have kept the secret too long, my Queen. I will inform Troy immediately," he said. "I'm trying to leave my past behind."

"Shady Grove is just the place for that, but I suggest you start over with the truth," I said with my hands on my hips.

"Yes, of course. You're right," he said.

"You hear that, Levi?" I asked teasing my bard. I loved being right. I loved hearing the words even more. My tease to Levi had been to lighten him up, but it didn't work.

"Yes," he grumbled.

I giggled as Dominick left the bar in a hurry. When I turned back to Nestor and Levi, my grandfather's smile was wide, but he shook his head at me. Levi refused to look at me.

"I'm sorry. I assumed..." Levi started to say as I lightly ran my hand over his tattooed arm. He gulped and shivered. I was sexually charged up, and he could feel it.

Raising up to my tip-toes, I planted a kiss on Levi's cheek. He huffed, then sighed. I could hear Nestor chuckling as he moved away from us. Without pulling away from his face, I whispered, "You're adorable when you're jealous."

"Damn, Grace," he muttered.

I smiled, then sat back down on my stool to finish my coffee while Levi gathered his senses.

He took a long sip of the coffee the muttered again, "Damn."

"You okay?" I asked as Nestor poured a second cup of coffee.

"I'm sorry," he said.

"Levi, don't ever apologize for caring about me," I said trying to let him off the hook.

"I felt you upset earlier, and I tried to give you space, but I found myself following you here. I felt the change in you when you touched him. I should have known you were up to something," he explained.

"I was upset earlier, but you don't have to stay away. I never asked for that," I said knowing that he felt a need to respect my relationship for Dylan and the loss I felt. But Levi had always been my rock. It was difficult walking the line between respect for the past and the needs of the present. My instincts were to move closer to Levi, not further away. To me, our connection had always been wholly separate from Dylan. In a way, I think Dylan knew that. He practically blessed any future contact between Levi and me.

One thing was for sure, neither of us was ready to fall down that rabbit hole. In the meantime, I just wanted it to be less awkward between us.

"Why were you upset earlier?" he asked.

"I drove past the spot out at the creek where Dylan and I liked to picnic. I pulled over and got out hoping to feel closer to him. To remember. It was too much," I said. "But I tucked away the grief and came here for some coffee."

As he sipped on his coffee, I felt his demeanor calm. The matured bard returned with each drink. Sometimes I missed the emotional, impulsive Levi. The new one was more attractive though. Not that I needed any more encouragement in that department.

"He loved that spot, too," he said. Somewhere along the way, Dylan had shared that with Levi. I supposed it was when he told Levi his side of our story. "You don't have to hide your grief, Grace. No one will think you're weak for mourning him."

"I'll mourn him after I kill Robin," I said gritting my teeth.

"You can do both," he suggested.

"I can't get distracted," I said.

"Pain isn't a distraction. It's fuel. Use it," he said.

"I'm afraid to let it take any part of me. It will be too much for me to handle," I said admitting my fears.

He placed his hand over mine rubbing his thumb over my skin. The song he played through his tattoo didn't play audibly, but I could feel it through his fingers on mine. The calming sensation of the song with the added coffee, plus a fairy tingle, and my senses were overloaded.

"That's why I'm here. For when it's too much," he said.

"Damn," I muttered echoing his earlier sentiment. I turned my hand palm up lacing my fingers through his. The pounding in my heart couldn't be compared to the thump from Dominick's flirt. Not even close.

CHAPTER SEVENTEEN

As I buttered Nestor up to talk to Mable, Levi sat quietly allowing me to work my charm on my Grandfather. Finally, he piped up to offer an alternative.

"Why don't you come upstairs and look through her stuff," he said. "You might find something useful."

"Wouldn't hurt," Levi said.

I agreed in hopes that it would push Nestor to go and talk to Mable.

Nestor led Levi and me upstairs into his apartment. Mable had moved in with him not long after I became aware of their relationship. While she worked at the Food Mart, she constantly stirred up gossip. Particularly when she told me what Dylan had said about me to his guy friends. That one act kept us apart longer than it should have. I couldn't blame her though, because I had turned a cold heart to Dylan at the time. I was looking for an excuse to ignore my feelings.

"You sure you don't mind if we look through her stuff?" Levi asked, then took a sip of the beer Nestor had opened for him downstairs. I hadn't seen him drink the piss water in a while. We didn't keep it in the house, but perhaps I should buy him some.

"No. I want you to go through it. If you find something that will help with the war or with the witches, it will help all of us here," he said. "Just be careful of the big trunk. It's got a spell on it. I touched it once and my finger was numb for days."

"I'll handle it," Levi said.

"I'm gonna laugh when it zaps you," I said.

"Oh, ye of little faith," he said.

Levi had proven he had all sorts of skills in the magical department, but Mable was a formidable witch. Part of me hoped he didn't get hurt, but the other part was prepared to have a good laugh.

Nestor took us into his bedroom where in the corner there was a shrine to the goddess. A banner hung from the corner depicting the Celtic tree of life. It was a deep hunter green with a golden knotwork. A small table sat in front of it with various candles. In the center, a wreath made of grapevines encircled a pentacle made of sticks and twine. A statue of the goddess stood in the center. Three women back to back forming a triangle: maiden, mother, and crone. Two wooden bowls held herbs and a goblet sat off to the side. Another bowl was filled with crystals of various colors and sizes. It all looked pretty standard for the practice of witchcraft.

When looking through my sight, I could see the faint glow of magic surrounding it. I was surprised to see that the magic was not black, but a dark green. However, the trunk sitting beside the table glowed brightly with the ward which protected its contents.

"I dunno, Levi. Looks pretty tough to me," I said.

"For you maybe," he said.

"Go ahead. I wanna see your cocky ass get fried," I said.

Nestor chuckled at my ribbing of Levi. Nothing made me feel more like myself than giving Levi a hard time. And since I knew he loved every minute of it, I promised myself to do it more often. It was good therapy.

"She kept all her clothes in there," Nestor said pointing to the small closet.

I opened the door to see the clothes we had seen her wear ever since I'd known her. Nothing looked out of place, and none of it had any evidence of magical echo.

"Did Mable do the concealment spell for Betty?" I asked.

"She did," Nestor answered. "She concealed herself pretty well too. I should have known better."

"The heart wants what the heart wants," I said.

"It didn't start out like that. It was more of a mutual release of pent-up frustration," he said.

"T.M.I.," I said as Levi laughed. I kicked him in the shin.

"Ow! Damn," he whined.

"You're a pain," I said.

He laughed again. "I'm gonna show you that I can do this," he said moving over to the trunk.

"Just don't get your junk in the way. I'd hate that to go numb on you," I said.

"It's not like I'm using it," he mumbled. Nestor covered his forehead with his hand and shook his head. "Here. Hold my beer."

"Famous last words," I said, taking the bottle from him. "I don't know how you drink this shit. It stinks."

"You get used to it," Levi said concentrating on the trunk.

Levi pulled power from the room around us. He had an uncanny ability to pull power inside as well as outside. I'd only known the highest born fairies to be able to do that. I supposed it was the gift of Taliesin that my father had given him.

"Dispel," he simply said. "Okay. You can open it."

"Oh, hell no! You open it," I instructed.

"Fine," he huffed. He reached for the metal latch which would have held a lock if it had needed one. As his hand touched it, he screamed, falling backward from the box. He rolled on the floor howling in pain.

"Shit!" I exclaimed, falling to my knees next to him.

Rocking back and forth he bellowed, "Oh, shit. Oh, shit. Oh, shit."

"What is it? What's wrong? Talk to me, Levi," I said starting to panic.

He stopped rolling, opened his eyes, and grinned.

"Awe, Grace, you care," he said.

Nestor howled in laughter.

"Levi Rearden, you're so full of shit. I'm gonna stomp a mudhole in yo' ass," I yelled as I started slapping at him. He defended himself by putting his arms in front of his face, but it didn't stop his laughter.

"Mercy, Grace! Mercy," he said, trying to catch his breath.

"No mercy for lyin' tricksters!" I protested. Relenting my assault, I rolled back on my heels to get up when he grabbed my hand. "Let go of me."

"It's good to see ya all riled up," he said.

"Let go of me, you fool," I said. He rubbed my hand just before letting go sending tingles through my body.

As he got up off the floor, he and Nestor continued to giggle. Heathen.

Levi flipped open the lid. In the very center, a tray stretched across the trunk, holding a bright red cloak laid.

"You never saw this?" I asked Nestor.

"I've never seen it open," he replied.

Levi picked up the tray. The trunk was filled with all sorts of jars and boxes. Anything a witch would need to cast a spell. None of it looked out of the ordinary. The ingredients themselves weren't magical. It was the correct combinations of them that could produce potent spells.

Levi dug through the trunk. The last item he pulled out was a worn leather tome. Every witch had a book of spells. I was interested to see exactly what spells Mable kept in her book.

We sat down on the edge of the bed as Nestor backed out of the room.

"Where are you goin'?" I asked.

"I don't want to know, Grace," he said sadly.

"Alright," I said feeling bad for him. He hadn't noticed her activities, and it hurt him. I wished I could ease the pain, but I didn't know how.

"He will be okay," Levi said reading my thoughts.

He flipped through a few pages of the spell book. It was like a diary of the spells she had cast and gathered over the years. As we turned the pages, the spells became more complex. However, most of them were still benevolent in nature.

Towards the end of the book, Mable had recorded in spells to summon demons and other beings of nefarious intentions. There was a spell to contain an aswang. Levi pointed it out.

"She knew about Lysander," he said.

"It seems so," I said.

Turning to the next page, I gasped and jumped off the bed.

"Fuuuuuck," Levi said. "This is how to make the Absinthe truth moonshine."

"Yes. The trailer that exploded was full of it," I said. "I bet she's the one that planted the fields."

"Wow," he said.

I watched across the room as he flipped pages. "This one is a glamour to make a child look like the offspring of someone else," he said. "Like how Devin looked like Dylan."

"This bitch is something else," I said. "I'm not sure I want to know anymore. Put the book in the vault. I don't want anyone else to have it."

Staring at the page, he shuddered. When his eyes lifted to mine, I saw the terror in them.

"What?" I asked.

He looked back down at the book. He read, "After many contacts, I've finally reached the conclusion that the only way to terminate the bard would be to trick the Queen into exterminating him herself. Considering their blood bond, she is the only one that could break through his vast power which is not likely to happen. Except the chance that we could get the Phoenix to do it."

"That's why they brought the jar to the bonfire," I said. "They wanted you dead."

"Why me?" he asked.

"You're damn powerful if you haven't noticed. They are scared of you because they know you will protect me. That you will protect Shady Grove," I said.

"Nothing like a big fat target on your back. Where'd my beer go?" he asked.

I picked it up, handing it to him. He took a long draw off if it as he looked at the words that had planned his demise.

"They won't stop trying to find ways to stop us," I said.

"Let them waste their time. They ain't stopping us," he said.

I smiled because his determination warmed my heart. Levi had long left Texas behind as his home, but among the other changes in our lives, I knew he belonged here.

"I'm going to convince Nestor to talk to her," I said.

"I'll take this to the vault. Pick me up on your way," he said.

CHAPTER EIGHTEEN

NESTOR AGREED TO MEET WITH MABLE, BUT IT WAS RELUCTANTLY.

"I don't know that I can sway her," he said. "Besides what do you want to know?"

"I want to know how she got the jar. What these ORCs have planned? Who is the third?" I said rattling off all the questions in my head about the red cloak gals. One thing I knew for sure. I couldn't wait to turn each one of them to icy dust.

"I can try," he said.

"I don't mean to hurt you," I said. He was riding in the back seat of the truck while Levi drove us to the holding cell.

"I know you don't, but I love her. I was blinded, and I'm ashamed of that. All those years I spent disliking Dylan for being blinded by a fairy queen, here I was blinded by a witch," he said. "I knew she had spied for your father, but I had no idea that she had turned on us."

"I should have known when you showed us the talisman against the evil eye," I said. "It was too convenient."

"We even talked about it," Levi said.

"Yep. And I was blinded too," I said.

"We all were," Levi added. It didn't make Nestor feel any better.

Something about sleeping with the enemy made it that much worse for him. Good thing he didn't know who all I had slept with in my day. He had nothing to be ashamed of. Levi didn't look at me, but he lifted an eyebrow.

Just the simple gesture of holding his hand had set him into a good mood. After Nestor suggested we go upstairs to search Mable's stuff, he gently let go with a silent thank you. The problem was it gave him hope. Not that Levi and I weren't on some collision course, for better or for worse. But I didn't want anything between us to be because Dylan had a dream or because Levi was attached to me because of his love-talker heritage. It was a convoluted mess that made my head hurt.

When we pulled up to the cell block, Troy exited the building.

"Afternoon, Grace. Come to talk to the prisoner?" he asked.

"Yes. Well, Nestor is going to give it a go," I said.

"She's getting antsy in there. She might talk just to get out," Troy said.

"She is never getting out," I replied.

"Why?" Nestor asked. "What has she done? Did she kill anyone?"

"Remember that fire at Hot Tin? Right when we were on the trail of Lysander's activities? She knew I had found out about our relationship. She knew it would distract me. She almost killed you," I said.

"She nursed me in the hospital," Nestor said.

Love is so damn blind.

"Yeah, none of us ever suspected her," I said.

"She didn't," he said.

"Ask her," I said pointing to the door.

I saw the look in his eyes. He knew I was right. I think perhaps he thought this Order of the Red Cloak gig was a recent one, but from my perspective, she had been at it for a very long time. The old crone. Gossiping in the grocery store. Stirring the people of Shady Grove up. Collecting various spells that pertained to everything that had happened in Shady Grove over the last year.

We followed him inside. Just before he walked into the back with the cells, I stopped him. I put my hand on his arm.

"I love you. You're so important to me. I want to rip her guts out for hurting you, but if I do it, I promise it will be quick for your sake. For now, I need information," I said.

"I love you too, Grace. And I understand. I don't have to like it, but I understand," he said, bowing his head, then disappearing into the cell block.

"You can listen over here," a female voice came from behind us.

"Amanda, hello," I said.

"Sorry. Wolves can be sneaky," she smiled.

She led Levi and me into a room adjacent to the cells. Cameras were set up to look into each cell from separate directions.

"Has this always been here?" I asked, knowing I'd spent a couple of nights in the cells.

"Yes," she smiled. "I sat here and watched as you sent him away."

"He was so damn persistent," I said.

"He loved you, and he wouldn't give up. We knew he was staying in the trailer with you, but we decided to leave it. We could have used it to fire him. Of course, I was an idiot and got into that whole mess on the wrong side," she said.

Thinking of those memories saddened me. It was time that he and I should have been together, but I was too stubborn to see what my heart felt.

We turned our attention to Nestor who approached Mable in the cell. She sat on the bed looking at him as he walked up. He grabbed the folding chair from against the wall, placing it near the cell.

"I want to go in there the moment she steps out of line," I said.

"You better let me do it," Levi said. "Unless you're ready to put her down."

"You act like I can't control myself," I said.

"That's Nestor in there. Your grandfather. If she does something to him, I will be the only one that can stop you from killing her. So, you tell me now what you want," Levi said.

I paused to think it over. She eyed Nestor who had begun to ask her if she needed anything. "I trust your judgment," I said.

He nodded, and we listened in to the conversation.

"I don't want anything from you," she said staring at him. "You're here for her. Not for me."

"I *am* here for her. She is my blood. You should tell her what you know. Perhaps she will spare your life," he said.

"If I tell her what I know, she will tie me to a stake and burn me," Mable countered.

The thought had crossed my mind.

"Have you always lied to me?" he asked.

"I never lied to you. I am a witch. You always knew that," she said.

"Did you burn my bar and home down?" he asked.

She didn't need to answer. I saw the look in her eyes. Unfortunately, Nestor did too. He stood up from the chair silently folding it to place against the wall. He couldn't ask her any more questions. I didn't blame him. Just before he hit the door, she called out to him.

"Nestor."

He paused.

"I regret it," she said.

"It's too late for regret after you've been caught," he replied. "I don't want to ever see you again." He passed through the doors, and I ran out to meet him. I folded him up into a big hug. He held on tightly.

"I'm so sorry," I said.

"It's not your fault," he replied.

"Sometimes we can't see the forest for the trees," I said.

"That's advice you could take too, Gracie."

I wasn't sure what he meant until I felt Levi walking up behind us. Big fucking tree.

"We are fine," I said.

"You could be better," Nestor said.

"War. Big, fat, freaking war coming," I said.

Nestor smiled. "I know."

"Let me have a round with her. I need to work off some frustration," I said.

"*I could…*" Levi started.

"Don't you dare!" I said spinning around to point at him. I tried to be mad, but the ridiculously cocky look on his face cracked me up. "Damn it. Stop."

"I didn't say anything," he shrugged.

"I'm going to talk to the witch now," I said.

"You do that," he replied.

"I will. I mean, I am."

CHAPTER NINETEEN

WHEN I CAME THROUGH THE DOORS, SHE ROLLED HER EYES AT ME. Usually, I was on the giving end of that gesture. I never realized how annoying it was to receive it. Between being pissed off at her and frustrated with Levi, I was sure this conversation was going to lead to nothing productive, but I'd see if I could provoke her into saying something that would help us identify the third witch.

"I get it," I said.

"Don't play with me, Grace," she said.

"No, seriously, I get it. You followed your agenda plus ate cookies out of the jar. Then your hand got stuck. That stinks," I said.

"You may think that I don't care for him, but I do. I just hoped that one day he would see things differently," she said.

"I'm all about different," I said.

"You don't get it either. It's the whole system of queens and kings. The elites vs. the lowly," she said. I didn't know where she stood in that hierarchy but considering that she worked for my father automatically put her under his thumb.

"You think you're fighting for the little guy?" I asked.

"Yes," she smiled, seeming quite self-satisfied.

"You're wrong. My goal is to teach the little guy to fight for himself. No one needs a queen or a king. Just a big freaking family to back each other up. That's what I am about. You were a part of that. At least I thought you were," I said.

"You sound disappointed," she said.

"I am. In myself for trusting you, but I'm all about trusting someone until they prove me wrong," I said.

"Then what?" she asked.

"I extinguish them with extreme prejudice," I replied. "You're on my list."

"I'm not afraid of you," she said.

I skipped inside the cell, then pushed her against the wall. Sneering in her face, I allowed the winter to fill the cell. Ice formed on the floor, and she barely held her footing. I saw the fear in her eyes. That dark part of me laughed at it. The ice attached to her legs was crawling up to her thighs as it encased her.

"And I thought fairies couldn't lie," I smirked.

"*Grace.*"

"*I'm fine.*"

"I'll never betray them," she said.

"That's fine. You can rot," I said, releasing the spell, then skipping back to the door. "Goodbye, Mable. The next time I see you, you will either tell me what I want to know, or I will kill you. If you change your mind about squealing, send word."

She started to speak, but I closed the door to the cells. I meant it. She would either tell me or not. It was up to her. No more torture.

Levi followed me out of the compound without saying a word. He was getting awfully good at learning to keep his mouth shut. When he didn't though, I had to listen. I slowed my march to the truck and turned back to see his face. I cared about what he thought of me. He walked straight up to me with a solemn look.

"I am always on your side," he said.

"There is still a part of me that wants to beat the answers out of her. The other part of me wants to throw in the towel, take my children, and run," I said.

"Too late for that," he said.

"Yeah. Way too late," I said.

"Nestor is waiting in the truck. We should go," he said. His phone buzzed in his pocket. "Hello?"

It sounded like Tennyson on the other end.

"She's with me. We are on our way, but we will have to drop Nestor off at the bar," he said.

"What is it?" I whispered.

"Okay. See you in a few," Levi said, hanging up. "He said he has something and needs to see us immediately."

"Good or bad?" I asked.

"He didn't sound happy," Levi said.

"Well, shit."

CHAPTER TWENTY

Tennyson paced the room as Levi and I sat waiting on Astor and Troy to arrive. Mr. Mob Boss had always been the calm, collected one, but tonight he was on edge. Astor had called Ella to watch the kids while we had this impromptu meeting. I needed a permanent babysitter, on retainer.

"Tennyson, what's going on?" I asked impatiently.

"We will wait for the others," he said.

"Grace, they need to be here," Jenny coaxed. "Perhaps I can get you a drink. I have orange soda."

"Crown. On the rocks," I said.

"Me too," Levi said as his leg jiggled nervously beside me.

With a sudden burst of light, Astor stepped through a portal created by his sword. His brow tensed when he saw Tennyson's face.

"What is it, Brother?" he asked.

"Sit. We wait," Tennyson said as he made another line across the floor. Jenny turned her attention to him after serving us drinks.

"Please. Don't do this to yourself. We will handle this like we do everything else. Okay?" she said pressing her palm to his cheek. The gruff man softened at her touch, leaning into her palm.

"Yes, my Love," he replied.

Astor bowed his head, not focusing on the exchange. I had noticed that all intimate moments like this bothered him.

"Call him," I said.

"He's almost here," he said.

The lights of a car flashed across the room, and the engine of Troy's cruiser cut off. When he came in, my brother, Finley was with him.

"What's going on? Glory, are you okay?" Finley asked.

"I'm fine. He called the meeting," I said, pointing at Tennyson. I had called Finley, but he didn't answer. I had hoped he would get my message in time to meet us.

Tennyson sighed, then took a seat in the large leather chair across the room. Jenny followed him perching herself on the arm of the chair. He wrapped his mammoth arm around her waist.

"My contacts in Winter believe that Brockton has found a way to breach the ward, and after a little research, I believe that he can," he said.

"How?" Levi asked.

"Samhain approaches. The veil between the worlds will weaken. It's what brought the ghouls here to collect Betty," he said. I hadn't told him about Betty, so I wasn't sure how he knew about it. Luther hadn't joined us tonight, but I got the impression he was on strict house arrest. Or bottle arrest until Betty's fury settled. She hadn't given me her decision on my proposal. "Perhaps it can be stopped but I've never known it to stop for anyone."

"What? What can be stopped?" I pressed.

"The hunt. Brockton is summoning the Wild Hunt to cross the veil at Samhain into Shady Grove and ransack it," he said. "It cannot be stopped."

The tales of the hunt frightened me when I was younger. I looked down to see chill bumps raise up on my skin as if a haint had crossed my path. Levi looked down at my arm, then up to me. He knew that nothing shook me, but this did.

"We should make preparations to move as many people away from the city as possible," Astor said. "Grace, your children should be sent away."

"I'm not sending my kids anywhere," I said.

"You should go with them," Troy added.

"No," I growled. "I will not leave. We fight. We will show him that he can pull all the ancient tricks out of the book. We are writing our own story. This Samhain the Hunt dies."

Tennyson hung his head. My speech did nothing to persuade him. Jenny squeezed his hand, then began to speak.

"It's not that easy. Your father used to lead the Hunt with his sword. If he is summoning the hunt, then he has Excalibur. We always thought that Nimue would give it to you, but apparently she has chosen someone else," she said.

"Can it be summoned without the sword?" I asked.

"Yes," Levi said.

"No, it cannot," Tennyson shot back at him.

"Yes, it can. It's in the book," he countered. The tattoo on his arm flared and the single word he spoke shook the house. "Book."

The Songbook of Taliesin appeared in his open palms. He stuck his finger in the book, turning to the passage. He began to read.

"When the veil grew thin, a great horn blew and the hounds bellowed. The wind swirled around the Great King as he raised his sword. 'Come to me my fallen. Come to me, oh ye of the wilds. Let us band together to defeat those who would disgrace our name!' An eerie cry filled the air as the grey woman keened for the dead. One by one the specters rose from hill and dale across the moors. Shadows and smoke formed in the mists of the night. They joined together behind their King swarming the hills in darkness. The thunderous echoes of their forgotten steps bounced off each tree, rock, and bush. The dead had risen to ride in vengeful wrath. Those who stood in their way were fodder below their feet. Foot, hoof, and paw. They ran through the forest and the town taking as they wished. A reminder of their lives for those who had forgotten. When the hunt rode, no man or fairy escaped its fury."

"Levi, the Great King was Arthur and the sword was Excalibur. It had many names, but my King called it Excalibur," Tennyson said.

I leveled my eyes at him, and he winced. "It is not the King and the sword that call the hunt. It was the horn and the banshee plus other elements mentioned. I just happen to know a banshee. This town is full of foot, hoof, and paw. Whatcha wanna bet we can call our own hunt?"

"Forgive me, Levi," Tennyson said.

Levi waved his hand, but I felt the burning inside of him to set Tennyson straight. He deferred to his teacher, but I didn't have to defer to shit. I held my fury in check, trying to endeavor to be a better, less impulsive person.

"You may be on to something, Grace," Astor said. "We could call our own hunt, but it still boils down to a leader with a sword riding a horse. Do you ride? Because I know you said that you aren't a sword fighter."

I didn't answer him. My mind went in twenty different tangents, but it all boiled down to one thing. I knew what I had to do.

"Come on, Levi," I said, standing up.

"Where are you going?" Tennyson asked.

"To prepare for our hunt. The hunt of the Exiles," I replied, then blinked out of the room to Trailer Swamp.

Levi jumped right behind me. "Why are we here?"

"Do you feel her in the water?" I asked, looking at the dark water of the bog.

"Yes," he replied.

"Let's play with the swamp monster," I grinned.

CHAPTER TWENTY-ONE

S<small>HIFTING TO MY UBER QUEEN FORM.</small>

~

"Uber queen form?" Grace asked, reading over my shoulder.

"Yeah. You like? I asked.

"No, Levi. Are you typing everything I say or typing your own story?" she asked.

"I'm just making it exciting," I replied, taunting her just a little bit.

"Did you type the part earlier where I said I was going to knock you into next week?" she asked.

"Yes," I replied.

"Good. Type it again for right now," she smirked. "And get that uber shit out of there."

"Okay," I groaned.

~

Shifting to my winter queen form, the glowing tattoos crossed my body in swirls. My dress shifted to the black mourning dress, and I called out to the creature in the swamp.

"Melusine, I am Grace Ann Bryant, Queen of the Exiles, Daughter of Oberon, come forth," I called out into the darkness. The water stilled without a ripple. The moon was hidden by thick clouds, and the shadows cast upon shadow.

"You know her name?" Levi whispered.

"Apparently. It's like I only remembered it just now," I said.

"Like everything else," he muttered. "She's moving closer."

"Melusine, I command thee as an inhabitant of my realm to speak to me!" I yelled.

The black sheet of glass didn't move, but the katydids and frogs ceased their song.

"She is there," Levi said. He was afraid. I could feel it in him. I didn't have time to explain to him who she was, but I knew now that she wouldn't hurt me despite what happened to my trailer. She wasn't after me that day. It was much clearer now that I knew about the ORCs.

"Melusine, I'm not going to ask again. Get your water serpent ass out here," I yelled.

"I don't think serpents have asses," Levi quipped, using humor to mask his fear.

"Shush," I said as the water rippled. I stepped to the edge. Levi lunged toward me to grab my arm.

"What are you doing?" he said with panic in his eyes. "I've pulled you out of there once."

"And if I need you to do it again, you will," I countered.

He huffed, then released my arm. "Just don't. Please."

The water exploded before us showering us in a thick mist of swamp water. A large serpent raised out of the water, but her head and torso were *all* woman from her navel to her bare breasts to her head. Her lower body was covered in scales with tiny suction cups on the bottom side like an octopus. She had fins along the back of her body down to a tail shaped like a mermaid which slapped the water.

"You don't own me, little Queen," she said towering above us.

"Holy crap," Levi said.

She rose higher and higher out of the water looking down at us from nearly 10 feet.

"Not technically, but this is my town. I could make you leave," I said.

"I guard the waters. I cannot leave," she protested.

"What are you guarding?" I asked. I knew, but I asked anyway. I was in a very provocative mood tonight.

"To be a Queen, you seem to be ignorant," she said as she slithered back and forth on her tenti-tail. If she wasn't half fish snake, she would be beautiful. Perhaps that was my folly. It didn't matter that she had a weird bottom end. She was beautiful nonetheless. I changed my approach. "You weren't always like this, were you?"

She paused batting her eyelids in confusion. "I can change," she said.

"Show me," I said.

"*Please*," Levi prompted.

"*Stop doing that*," I replied to him. "Please."

Her tail shifted, splitting in two to become two tails. She raised up on the ends then took two steps. A radiant young woman stood before us. Cascading yellow hair, bright green eyes, and milky smooth skin. It was green, but it was smooth nonetheless. Levi cleared his throat, shifting his feet nervously behind me.

"*Don't act like you've never seen a naked woman*," I said.

"*They weren't half-snake, half-fish, half-women either*," he replied.

"*That's too many halves. What are they teaching our kids in school these days?*" I said.

"*Grace!*" he scolded.

I swung around on him, and he was already backing away from me with his hands up in surrender. "Sorry. My bad," he said. Chicken.

"He's cute," she said.

"He's mine," I said quickly.

"*What?!*"

"*Shush*," I said.

"*No, no, no, no. What did you just say?*"

"Levi Rearden, I swear to the goddess if I knew your middle name I'd use it right now," I said in frustration. The fish woman watched us exchange looks without speaking.

"You should know my name, Grace," he said.

"You've never told me," I said.

"You never asked," he replied.

"What is it?" I asked.

"Not now," he replied.

"Levi!"

He waved my attention back to Melusine who tilted her head trying to figure out what was going on between us.

"We are connected. I can hear him in my head," I said.

"Oh! I see. Forgive me for insinuating something about your mate," she said.

Levi laughed.

"Shut up!" I said. Melusine took a step backward. "Oh, no. Not you, honey. That man back there can be distracting."

"You have no idea," he said.

I took a deep breath determined to ignore him. "I'm sorry. Now, can you tell me what you're guarding?" I asked.

"The grand-daughter of the Queen of Summer requested that I guard these waters because she heard that the invasion from the exiles would be made through the mists into Avalon. This is the outskirts of the mists," she said.

"No, honey. This is just Alabama," I said.

"Is that near Avalon?' she asked.

"Close enough," I replied.

"Oh, well. You and your usurpers' plot has been discovered. You will enter Avalon through these waters, and although I am sorry, I will have to kill you should you try," she said.

"I won't try," I replied. It was the truth. Up until now, I didn't realize the significance of the waters. Robin had created a portal like the hedge maze and the church into the Otherworld through the swamp that devoured my trailer. "Is my trailer still down there?"

"It is, but I don't think it is salvageable," she said.

I thought of all the things I lost when the trailer went down, however, none of them were as important as my family. That was really the day I lost Dylan. We rushed headlong into the situation without thinking about the consequences. That's what I was doing in provoking the Lady of the Lake, but if Brockton was calling for the hunt, he would be calling it through these mists. A portal created by Robin. His current wife.

"The important things are still with me," I said. "Look. We got off on the wrong foot. I received some distressing news about the thinning of the veil, and I must speak with the Nimue as soon as possible. Do you have a way to contact her?"

"Yes, I do, but you promise that it is an emergency?" she asked.

"Yes," I replied.

"Very well. Wait here," she said as she stepped back from me. She flipped backward shifting into the fish-snake woman and swam off into the deep.

I put my hands on my hips and turned to Levi. "What the hell has gotten into you?"

"I dunno," he shrugged.

"What is your middle name?" I asked.

"We aren't having this discussion now," he smiled.

Wanker. Fine. I could play dirty too. I shifted the black dress to the revealing silver one that I favored. It was sequined trailer trashy. Four-inch heels and a look to kill, I stalked toward Levi who raised an eyebrow but didn't budge. I traced a long nail up the guitar tattoo, and he groaned.

"Grace," he said through gritted teeth.

"Tell me your middle name," I said.

He narrowed his eyes at me, and I felt a shift in him. The seduction held no power, but he stepped toward me. I almost stumbled on the heels as I moved to make room between us. He continued to step until I reached the edge of the water.

"Not. Right. Now," he said defiantly.

If the water hadn't parted, I would have...

"Would have what?" I asked, interrupting her narrative.

"Done something," she said.

"Oh! I'm scared," I mocked.

"Type, bard boy," she said, pointing at the laptop.

"Bard man. Thank you very much. Don't make me prove it to you," I replied.

To that, she grinned. "May I continue?"

"Of course," I said hovering my hands over the keyboard.

"Tell me how you would prove it," she said.

"Not now, Grace," I said, wiggling my suspended fingers.

She rolled her eyes, then continued the story.

A female cleared her throat behind me.

"Oh, Nimue, sorry. Just having a little discussion with my bard," I said, turning to face her. Levi stood right behind me, and I swore he breathed down my neck just to make me wobble.

"Did I interrupt something?" she asked.

"Nothing important," I replied.

I expected Levi to comment, instead, he put his hand on my bare back. This dress was a bad idea.

"You summoned me?" she continued.

"I did," I said trying to gather my thoughts. "It seems as though my Uncle prepares to call for the hunt. However, I was under the impression, along with my knights, that the hunt required a king which he is not, and Excalibur, which I assume he also does not have. The last time I saw my Father's sword, you had it."

She waved her hand, and Excalibur rose up from the depths of the swamp. "This sword?" she asked.

"Yes, my father's sword," I replied. I could hear the power in the hum of the blade.

"Are you taking your Father's throne?" she asked.

"I am going to boot my Uncle from the Otherworld before he destroys it," I said.

She waved her hand again, and the sword sank into the depths.

She walked out of the water, and Levi pulled me back as she approached us. "I asked you a question, and like the impertenent child you have always been, you do not answer me!"

Levi pulled harder. *"No, we stand our ground,"* I said.

I felt him shifting power, then two glowing portal rings appeared. Astor and Troy stepped through one. Tennyson and Jenny stepped through the other. A roar rolled through the town as a giant winged shadow approached us. Luther landed down in all of his fiery glory between the other knights.

"An interesting show of force. Why do you call for backup, Bard?" she asked Levi.

"Loyalty in all battles," Levi replied.

The last to arrive, Finley, blinked in by our side in full armor with his sword raised. Nimue raised her eyebrow at him. "Finley, have you no objection to your sister ruling?"

"None," he replied.

"Shouldn't it be your throne as the male heir?" she asked.

"Male. Female. It doesn't matter. She is the right one for the job," he said.

"She cannot possibly wield your Father's sword," Nimue said. "All of you stand behind her despite her deficiencies?"

I watched her eyes cross behind Levi and I. I was sure by her look that everyone behind us gave her the nod of approval. It was time to make my move.

"You're right. I cannot wield Excalibur," I said. "But Levi can."

"No!"

"Yes," I replied softly.

"You have to rule. I don't want to rule. I'm here to support you," he argued.

"Ah, let's see how this goes," Nimue smiled. She knew I was talking to him. I turned my back on her to face Levi.

"The best thing you can do for me right now is to take up that sword. Not because I'm trying to prevent it from ending up with my uncle, but because I think you deserve it. The sword is not about ruling. It's about leading. You have shown that you know a few things about that during the time I wasn't paying attention, but I believe in you," I said.

His emotions twisted and turned inside of him. Despite the sword training and becoming the next Protector of the Vale, he doubted himself.

"Listen to me, Levi. You told me in the bar that you were here for me in the moments where it was too much for me to handle. That sword is too much for me," I said.

"Grace, that sword is legendary," he said, pointing over my shoulder to the swamp behind me.

"It is. One day, there will be people all over the Otherworld, Shady Grove, and beyond that will talk about the Bard who took up the sword and became a King," I said.

"She is right, Levi. I think it belongs with you," Tennyson said.

"Indeed," Astor echoed.

Levi stood silently as he searched through his thoughts and emotions. We had bantered and played, but I had turned the tables. His eyes finally met mine.

"She isn't offering it to me," he whispered.

I heard the waters shift behind me. I knew she had lifted the sword from the swamp once again.

"Let's see if you're worthy," she said.

The waters sloshed behind me, and I twisted to see that she had flung the sword across the street. It hummed as it flew over us, then embedded itself in a large rock which sat beside the "Welcome to Shady Grove" sign. It gleamed in the darkness.

Knowing the histories written by Taliesin, I knew the sword in the stone wasn't Excalibur, but the Lady in the Lake didn't seem to care about the old traditions. In a way, I supposed she did. She wanted Levi to prove himself. I also knew the sword chose the wielder, not the other way around.

"Tennyson, pull the sword," Nimue ordered.

"As you wish, Mother," he said. I had forgotten that the Lady of the Lake had raised Lancelot.

He walked over to the sword. His own hung from a sheath at his side. He removed his expensive suit jacket and handed it to Jenny.

She took it, then stepped away. Wrapping his tattooed hands around the hilt, he pulled. His muscles under his shirt flexed, but the sword did not move.

"I cannot pull it," he grunted as he tugged one last time. He nodded to Levi, then stepped back.

"Astor, pull the sword," Nimue ordered.

"I have no desire for the sword," he said with a bow.

"Pretend you do," she said urging him on. She was providing an object lesson for my bard. I knew he deserved it. I knew he was worthy or I would have never proposed it. She wanted him to see that none of these other knights deserved it. Even Virgin Astor.

Astor approached the sword. He bent his knees like a lumberjack that was in full swing with an ax while wrapping a red freckled paw around the hilt. He pulled with a grunt. His face turned the same color as his hair as he strained. The sword did not move.

"Would you like to try, Finley?" she asked. "Or either of you, wolf and ifrit?"

"No, my Lady," Finley responded.

I saw Troy and Luther shake their heads.

"It is left up to you, Levi Rearden," she said.

"Grace should try," he said.

This was going to take more convincing. "What if I take it up? Huh? When the hunt comes, can you see me standing on a battlefield, more than likely right here with that thing in my hands?" I asked holding my hands up to him. "They would mow me over if that were my weapon of choice. I choose you as my weapon. To stand with me when the veil thins and the darkness pours through. You have been a light for me since the moment you walked into my life. With that sword, you will be a beacon for all of us."

His emotions shifted again. When he looked up at me, I saw the boldness in his eyes. I had convinced him. Almost.

"You go get that sword before I jerk a knot in your tail!" I said.

"Damn, Grace," he grinned. His back straightened and his shoulders leveled. I saw the muscles in his arms flexing. He pulled no power into his tattoo. He played no song. He wanted to take the sword on his own, and suddenly I looked upon him as I had never allowed myself to do.

Up until this moment, I still saw that Levi who sat on my couch brooding because he'd been torn away from his witch girlfriend. A broken, confused boy. I had taken his devotion to me back then as a crush that would fade. However, it had grown into a friendship and a love that I had never expected.

My heart longed for the warm touch of Dylan, but it also saw the light that was the man that Levi had become. The Otherworld didn't break him. He made the hard decisions from a pure heart and a desire to do the right thing. It was why he didn't care about defying me when he was right, and I was wrong. He would protect this town no matter what Brockton threw at us. We would stand together to do it.

Back when he swore the blood oath to me, I didn't hesitate to make us equals. Some of our closest friends knew about that oath, but the sword would show all of the supernatural realms that I stood with him.

I believed that if I tried to pull that sword, it would come to me. It was mine by right.

Nimue spoke softly behind me, "As the King's daughter, yes, it would, but only if you accepted it as well. Your faith in him is unexpected."

"Surprised me, too," I whispered back.

Levi stood next to the stone with his eyes on the sword. *"Are you sure?"*

"Absolutely," I answered.

No stance or flexing required, Levi reached for the sword, and it jumped into his hand. A force of magic surged out of the ground beneath our feet rushing toward him. The glowing blue power ignited the sword like a shining beacon. His tattoo glowed with power as he stared at the sword in his hands. He turned toward me, holding it before him. His face was brightened by the light and magic swirled around his blue eyes. There would be no mistaking his power now. I just hoped he didn't form an ego. Our house was only big enough for mine.

Nimue passed me walking toward him. She lifted her hand and an ornate sheath appeared. I knew of the power of the sword, but the sheath also held the power to keep the bearer from being wounded. It had been lost longer than the sword. I never saw my father with it in the Otherworld. She had deemed Levi worthy of the entire inheritance.

"Take this, along with the sword. You have proven you're worthy today, but Excalibur demands that you continue to be so. If there ever comes the day, when you're unworthy, it will return to me. Blessings of the goddess to you, Levi Rearden, bearer of the Great Sword," she said.

Tennyson led the way as he dropped to one knee. The others quickly followed and Jenny bowed deeply. In respect, I lowered my eyes to the ground.

Nimue walked past me to the water as I continued to look down. Her feet hit the water's edge silently.

"Gloriana, daughter of Oberon," she called to me.

Turning to look at her, she smiled. "Yes, my Lady," I said with respect to her because I hadn't shown much from the beginning.

"Your ways are brash but crafty. As Excalibur deems Levi worthy, I deem you as well," she said raising her hand again. Out of the waters, the water stone which should have been in my vault hovered over her hand. The clear orb shifted with the glowing jewels inside. It floated across the air between us, stopping before me. I opened my palm as it settled into it. "You've never needed my approval to wield the water elements. You seem to be able to create your own snow at will. However, now, your spells will be blessed with the element of water and those of us who guard it. Not that you need any more power to win this war. Good luck to you."

"Thank you, Nimue," I replied.

She sank into the depths of the swamp as silently as she had come.

CHAPTER TWENTY-TWO

LEVI SLID THE SWORD INTO THE SHEATH, THEN LOOKED UP AT ME.

"I don't know what to say, but thank you, Grace," he said.

I reached up and touched the scar on his cheek. "I know that I give you hell, but I'm not an idiot to think I could do all of this on my own. We all have a role to play. This one is yours."

Tennyson slapped him on the shoulder. "Brother, welcome to the club."

"What club is that?" Levi asked.

"The named-sword club, of course," Tennyson replied.

"Oh?"

"This is Seure," Tennyson said, holding his sword up. "The Lady blessed all of our swords with the ability to open portals. But each has its own meaning to us."

"This is the Grail Sword. It was once broken, and I repaired it. Yet the crack remains as a reminder that even the strongest weapon has a weakness," Astor said.

We turned to Finley. "What? This old thing? I got it from our Father's vault when we were stealing stuff for Grace's vault."

"Children," Tennyson muttered.

Jenny popped Finley on the back of the head. "You, Moron. That's Galatine. It was given to Gawain by the Lady of the Lake."

"Oh, I thought it looked cool," Finley shrugged, but he looked upon the weapon with new eyes.

Luther stepped forward, revealing a sword tucked behind his wings. I hadn't noticed it before.

"This is Zulficar. It was given to a great man by Gabriel, the archangel. It was given to me after I was cursed as a weapon to prove my worth. I intend to do just that," he said with a smile. The sword tilted with an arching curve but split at the end like the long bill of a bird. It was downright scary. It matched Luther in his ifrit form perfectly.

We turned to look at Troy. He shrugged.

"I've got this," I said. Closing my eyes, I concentrated on the red car in my garage back home. As I lifted my hands, the box from the trunk appeared. I walked forward, then opened the box for him.

"No, Grace. I can't," he said.

"He would want you to have them," I said. "They are just sitting in the trunk of his car. They should be used."

Last Christmas, I had two Kimber 1911's made especially for Dylan. One featured a Phoenix and the other a Thunderbird. Dylan considered Troy to be like a brother. I knew he would want Troy to have them.

"It's not a sword," Troy pointed out.

"No, but they are your weapon of choice," I said. He ran his hands over the fine tooling of the guns. "I'm totally okay with this. Please take them."

"His children should have them," he said.

"Then, one day, when they are ready, you can give the guns to them," I said.

"Do they have names?" he asked.

I smiled and turned them over, showing him the D. Riggs engraved on the other side. "How about Driggs?"

"I like it. What does it mean?" he asked with a grin.

"It means badass muthafucka," I said.

Levi shook his head while the others laughed.

"He was rather impressive in Greece with those vamps," Luther said.

"I've heard that story. Too bad I don't remember the good parts," I said.

"I'd never seen anything like it," he said.

"Nor will you again," I replied.

"Never again," he said.

The mood turned very somber. "Don't be sad. He would have loved this moment. All of us coming together to fight the evil that threatens this town. It's what he did every day. We just have very big shoes to fill," I said.

"They were only size ten," Levi smirked. I swatted him on the shoulder.

"Jenny, do you have a sword?" I asked.

"No, actually, I was thinking that Nestor and I would be good candidates to protect your children while all of this is going on," she said. "Tennyson and I discussed it. As much as I would like to be fighting with you, I know that you cannot be focused on the battle while worried about your children. I suggest we take them, Mark, and the other kids into the vault. Mike can keep the outside safe, and we will take the kids inside. They will think it's a magical sleepover."

"I would like Ella to go with you," Astor said.

"Sure. She knows all the children from school. Hopefully, it will help to keep them calm if she is there," Jenny replied.

"What's going on with you and Ella?" I asked.

"Um, why do you ask?" he replied.

"Because for a moment, I could have sworn the two of you had an issue, but then not so much earlier," I explained.

"I asked her to marry me," he said.

"What?!" Levi and I said.

"I asked her, and she said she needed time to think about it," he said.

"Have you even kissed her?" I asked.

"I shall not tell," he said. The grin on his face told me everything.

"Is that all you did?" I prodded.

"Grace, leave him alone," Levi said.

"No! I gotta know!" I begged.

"She said yes," Astor deflected. It was a good deflection because a round of congratulations went around the group.

"*We should get home. How long do we have to prepare for this?*" Levi asked.

"*Samhain is the day after tomorrow,*" I said.

"*We have work to do,*" he said.

"*Yes, and I have a few ideas. We will visit Betty in the morning,*" I said.

When we stopped talking to each other, we realized they were all staring at us.

"Is there something on my face?" I asked.

"So, are you two?" Jenny asked.

"No!" we said.

"My B," Jenny replied. "You certainly don't have to talk about it with us."

"There is nothing to talk about," I said.

"There really isn't," Levi groaned.

"Oh, my goddess, let's go home," I said. "Keep preparing. We meet again tomorrow afternoon at the office."

Taking my hand, Levi said, "Home."

We stood in front of the house. When I started to walk inside, he tugged on my hand.

"Levi, I'm not sure I can talk about this right now," I said.

"I just want to know if you're okay," he said. "You gave his guns away."

"I had planned to give them to Troy. This just was the perfect opportunity," I replied. "I'm trying to be very strong, but if we start talking about it, I won't be able to hold it together."

"You need to let it out," he said.

"I did. The night he died. I won't do it like last time. After the trailer blew up, I laid in bed for days thinking he was dead. You weren't here, and I didn't know if you were alive. I spent too much time being weak while Aydan grew inside of me. I should have done better by him. I should have known Winnie wasn't safe. I locked myself away, and I just don't have time to do that now," I said.

"The difference is that I am here now," he said. "I wasn't before. I promise to keep you focused, but Grace, you need to just cry. Let it out. Hell, I loved him too."

"I do cry," I said.

"Silently. Alone. Don't you think I know that? Don't you think I feel it too?" he said.

"I know, but I don't want to cut you off. When you did that the other day it was awful. Don't ever do that again," I protested.

"I won't. I promise," he said. By the look in his eye, I knew he regretted it. It hurt him as much as it had hurt me.

"We won't always agree," I said.

"No, we won't," he said. "But that's okay, right?"

I looked down at my Father's sword hanging from his waist. I touched the end of it to feel the power in the sword. It was icy cold.

"You could have pulled the sword," he said.

"She said I could have," I said.

"I didn't learn to sword fight for this," he said. "I had no idea."

"It's good to know that I can still lock things away in my brain that you can't get to," I said.

"What?"

"I had always hoped to give it to you," I said.

"Not to Dylan?" he asked.

"What was Dylan going to do with a sword?" I asked. "He was a gun man all the way."

"What else do you have locked away in that brain of yours?" he asked.

"Come inside, and I'll tell you. The skeeters are going to eat me alive," I said.

As we walked into the house, he didn't let go of my hand, and I didn't want him to. Winnie ran up to us with hugs and kisses. We told her it was way past her bedtime. Ella had been watching them after Astor left to back us up at Trailer Swamp. She dismissed herself, hoping to find Astor before it got too late in the evening.

"He's peculiar about how late we are out together," she said.

"He's peculiar about a lot of things," I said.

"I'm easing him into new ideas," she said with a smile.

"Good for you, and good for him, too. I'm glad you said yes," I said.

"Me too," she blushed.

Levi took Winnie to bed while I checked on Aydan. When I opened the door, his little head bobbed up. A smile grew across his face, but his eyelids fluttered.

I rubbed the sandy blonde hair on his head. "Momma's home, Little Bird. Go back to sleep." His little lips puckered and he was gone again.

Shutting the door quietly, I stepped back into the hallway. Levi was turning the lights off in Winnie's room, then pulled her door closed behind him.

"She had a thousand questions about the sword," he said.

"What did you tell her?" I asked.

"I told her I was going to write a book about how I got it because she wouldn't believe it if I told her," he said.

"What? That you pulled it out of a stone? I'm pretty sure that story has been told," I said.

"No, that it was given to me by a Queen," he said.

"Damn you and your words," I said.

"I'm good, right?" he grinned.

"Then you go and ruin it," I laughed.

"Shh!" Winnie said from her room.

I put my hand over my mouth as I giggled. Levi moved closer to me then whispered, "It is so good to see you smile again."

"There are still things to be happy about," I said.

"Yes, there are," he replied with a smile. "Ready to talk about your plan?"

"It's not complete, but you can help me fill in the gaps," I said.

"I'll start some coffee," he said.

CHAPTER TWENTY-THREE

LEVI AND I SAT UP FOR HOURS DISCUSSING OUR OPTIONS FOR THE defense of Shady Grove. He looked up the tales of the Wild Hunt all across Europe. Each one had its own distinctions, but it followed the same thing. Bad things came and hurt good people. Not in my town. Wasn't going to happen.

We made a few changes to my original ideas as we read some of the information. Tomorrow, we needed to get the word out to the people of Shady Grove about the attack. I hoped we would have volunteers besides just my knights and me to defend the town.

Somewhere along the way, we fell asleep. I dreamed about the fight and our victory. I saw the last part of the plan come together in that dream. One last thing to keep from my bard. Only to surprise him later. It was something I didn't want to discuss, and once I revealed it, he would have no choice but to accept my decision. I just hoped it was the right one. However, I was sure that I'd regret it, right or not.

I jerked awake from the dream, finding my head resting on his chest. With the rise and fall of his breathing, I knew he was still sleeping. I had to calm my instincts to jump and run away from him. His right arm laid on my back with his hand at my waist.

I remembered the first time we slept in the same bed. We woke up with Winnie between us. The look he gave me that morning hadn't changed. He still looked at me like I was everything he ever wanted and a popsicle on the side.

Closing my eyes, I concentrated on maintaining my composure. We weren't doing anything wrong. Two friends. Sleeping on a couch. I shifted my weight, and his fingers curled into my side.

"You're awake," I said.

"I am now. What's wrong?" he asked.

"I just didn't expect to wake up like this," I said.

"You passed out on my shoulder, so I just shifted us, giving you a chance to rest," he said.

"I'm sorry," I said.

"Don't be sorry. I've been aching for the chance to just hold you, but you won't let me in. I know the boundaries, Grace. You can trust me," he said.

"I gave you my Father's sword," I said.

"Your heart, Grace. You can trust me not to make you uncomfortable or push. But you can also trust me to hold you close when you need to cry without getting any ideas," he said.

"No pushing? No expectations?" I asked.

"You know me better than that," he said out loud.

"Alright. What's your middle name?" I asked raising up to look him in the eye.

"I'm still hurt by that one. I'll have to see how long you beg before I tell you," he grinned.

"I'm gonna tan your hide!" I said.

"Oh, please," he begged.

I tried to get up, but he pulled me back down. I fought him harder, laughing the entire time. We both ended up on the floor wrestling, but he pinned me.

"What was that you were going to do?" he taunted.

"Don't make me go ice queen on you!"

"I ain't scared," he laughed.

"Are you going to kiss Mommy?"

Silence.

"Winnie!" Levi exclaimed rolling off of me. I raised up on my elbows to look at her sitting in the chair across the room holding a doll.

"Morning, Winnie," I said.

"Were you going to kiss Uncle Levi?" she asked.

"No. I was not," I said.

"Oh. It looked like it," she said. "You used to wrestle with daddy then you would kiss."

My heart sank, and I felt Levi's instant pain.

I rolled over to my knees and got off the floor.

"Grace," Levi called out to me.

"It's fine. She doesn't understand," I said, rushing to the kitchen. "Winnie, Uncle Levi and I were just goofing off. We are going to have a Samhain ceremony tonight. Are you excited?" I hoped if I changed the subject, she would too.

"Miss Jenkins has been teaching us about Samhain at school," Winnie exclaimed. "I'm so excited. It's like Halloween."

"It is," I replied as I washed out the coffee pot from last night. Levi returned our dirty mugs to the sink and took out three fresh ones.

"I don't think Astor is here," I said.

"Is he not?"

"I don't feel him here," I replied.

"Well, good for him," Levi said. Then he lowered his voice, "At least someone is getting laid."

I rolled my eyes at him, and he waggled an eyebrow. Fucking adorable. It was enough to shift my mood.

"Momma, can I dress up for Samhain?" Winnie asked.

A plethora of baby noises filled the room from upstairs. Most of them were of the variety of a notice that he was awake and alone in the room.

"I'll get him," Levi said dashing up the stairs to get Aydan.

"You're going to a special sleepover with Jenny, Miss Ella, and your Great-Grandfather," I said. "And you can dress up if you want."

"Yay! I want grits with cheese, please," she announced.

My mind wasn't on breakfast. It was on waking up with Levi,

and despite my panic, he treated it as something perfectly normal. He was trying not to freak me out. I took down a bowl to fix Winnie some grits. Pouring Levi and I a cup of coffee, I sat his out with the sugar. I generally drank mine black, but for some odd reason, I put two scoops of sugar in it. Not an odd reason. I was making coffee for Dylan.

Quickly, I poured my cup out in the sink and fixed a new one. Levi came down the steps with Aydan who was clapping and giggling at him.

"Go ahead, Aydan. Who's that?" he said pointing at me.

Aydan reached for me, opening and closing his little fingers. When I reached for him, Levi played his game.

"Who is it?" Levi coaxed.

Aydan just continued to reach for me but laughed each time Levi pulled him away.

"He's not going to say it," I said.

"He will," Levi said. "He's just a man of few words. Ain't that right, buddy?"

Aydan grinned at him.

"Unlike you, Bard. A man of too many words," I said.

"I'm not a man of *too many* words, Grace. I'm a man of the *right* words," he said.

"Your ego needs a deflate," I said.

"Nah. You always put me in my place," he said, finally letting Aydan come to me. He patted my face and gurgled something incoherent. I decided he said that he wanted to eat grits too. "Want some grits, Levi?" I knew the answer to that question.

"Really?" he said as he popped open his laptop at the dining room table.

"Never know when the man of the right words might have the right answer to that question," I said.

"Yeah, Uncle Levi. Grits are good," Winnie said climbing up in the chair next to him. "Oh, look. It's like your sword."

"Yes, it is," Levi said.

"What's this on the bottom?" she asked.

"That's the hilt, and those two creatures are chimera," Levi explained.

"Never heard of it," Winnie said.

"It's a mythological creature that has a lion's head and body. A goat's head comes out of its back, and its tail has the head of a snake on it. So, it can bite you," Levi said, grabbing Winnie and tickling her. The shrieks coming from her mouth could put Betty to shame.

Betty. She was going to be a key part of our plan. I just hoped the Banshee was ready to come out of retirement.

"Why are you looking up the sword?" I asked.

"Just finding whatever I can about it," he said.

"The songbook should have plenty about it," I said.

"It does," he replied. I knew that he had memorized the book, but he sometimes read over chapters when we needed a refresher. "I'm hoping to find something obscure. Something that might help us defeat Brock."

"Are you going to fight, Uncle Levi?" Winnie asked.

"Yes," he replied.

"I am going with him," I said. "Winnie, we have to stop this bad man."

"I don't want you to die," she said as her eyes welled up with tears.

"We aren't going to die, Winnie," Levi said. "We will always be here for you."

A promise made that he couldn't possibly keep, but that's what parents did every day. We lived each day protecting our children the best we could. When I looked at Levi showing Winnie things on his laptop to cheer her up and thought back to him playing with Aydan, it hit me that he not only was left here to take care of me but to be a surrogate father. He was too damn young to have to worry about such things.

"*Quit,*" he scolded me. "*We are family. That is all there is to it.*"

"*If I wanna get all up in my feelings, then let me,*" I said.

"*I can give you brooding lessons,*" he said.

"*No one does it like you do,*" I replied. I sat Aydan down at his chair with a bowl of grits and gave Winnie her bowl. She barely looked at it. "Eat."

"Yes, ma'am," she said, keeping her eyes on the screen, but reaching for her spoon.

"Can I get you something, Levi?" I asked.

"No, I'm not hungry," he said.

"Alright. I'm going to take a bath," I said.

"You are?" Levi asked.

"I am," I said. It had been too long. "Leave me alone."

"Gotcha," he said. "Winnie and I are going to do some fairy tale research."

I took one last look at them as I went up the stairs. The bath was to relax for a time because after it, there would be no more rest.

CHAPTER TWENTY-FOUR

AFTER GATHERING A FEW THINGS FOR MY BATH, I CLOSED THE DOOR to my bathroom which shut out a lot of the noise from downstairs. I hadn't so much as looked at the bathtub across the room for weeks. The shower and things were closer to the bedroom than the bath. When I approached it, I realized it had a box sitting in the bottom of it.

Warning bells went off in my head as I moved closer. The small box was wrapped in silver paper with a white bow. Someone had been in my bathroom. I eased closer, looking at the box through my sight. Someone with magical gifts had touched the box. It left a mark like fingerprints on it.

"*There is a box in my bathtub,*" I said.

"*Did you open it?*" Levi asked calmly.

"*No! I don't know how it got here!*" I protested.

"*Grace, open the box,*" he said.

I knew then who had been in my bathroom. Reaching down into the tub, I picked up the cube-shaped box. It was heavier than I expected. The ribbon fell to the floor after I pulled it open. Inside the box was a chalky orb that smelled like vanilla. A small note was inside the box, too. Unfolding the note, I recognized Levi's handwriting.

"*Grace, you have always been brave and beautiful to me. This is just one more step to living your life. You don't have to move on, but you do have to live. Enjoy the little things. With a bath bomb. All my love, Levi.*"

"Well, shit," I said, wiping tears. I'd seen these things on television and the videos that Winnie watched on her tablet. I started the warm water, then dropped the bomb into it. The swirling ball mesmerized me as it spun in the water giving off its heavenly vanilla scent. It was just like the perfume that I sometimes wore. I used to wear it all the time. I thought it masked my normal winter and apple scent. It reminded me of who I once was and who I had become.

There were days, even recently, that I was immature and rash. I toyed with Dylan's emotions. And even though, he enjoyed every moment of it, I felt like it was my fault we didn't have more time together. Of course, it also reminded me of Jeremiah who had kept us apart. I'd kill him if he weren't already dead. I needed to make sure I didn't toy with Levi's already too far gone emotions.

Dipping one foot into the tub, I could feel the warmth of the water through my cold skin. I sat back in the tub, letting the smell take over my emotions.

"*Thank you,*" I said.

"*You're welcome, Grace,*" he responded. Then he left me alone as I requested.

Sometime during my respite, Astor came home. I felt him enter while I was getting dressed. Levi and I needed to run some errands. I was glad he was here to watch the kids. Nestor would be here shortly, too. I wanted to let him in on the plan, so he would know my wishes if something happened to me. The thought caused me to pause, but I shook it off. We had to win. That was all there was to it. No exceptions. No hesitations.

As I exited my room, Levi came out of his freshly showered and dressed. I walked over and kissed him on the cheek. He blushed.

"Stay out of my bathroom," I scolded.

"Was it nice?" he asked.

"Different. Smelled good," I said.

"Good," he said. "Hey, go easy on Astor. He's not in a very good mood."

"What's wrong?" I asked.

"He didn't say," Levi replied. "Just give him a break for once."

"You act like I give him hell all the time. You must have him confused with you," I said.

"Maybe so," he grinned.

When I reached the bottom of the steps, Winnie was on the floor playing with Aydan. She had blocks which she built up, then he knocked down with a squeal each time. He had several teeth already, and that was when I decided to stop breastfeeding him. He had a terrible penchant for biting, and it hurt like the dickens. I missed that connection, but it was time to let it go.

His bright blue eyes followed the toys as Winnie rolled them around him. He looked up to see me, and I waved at him. He lifted his hand and waved back.

"Dear goddess, that was adorable," I said.

"I saw it," Levi said. "Cute."

I heard Astor in the kitchen muttering at the coffee pot. I looked back at Levi who shook his head at me. I couldn't help myself. Someone needed to find out what was wrong. If it had to be me, then so be it.

"Astor," I said.

"Oh, hi, Grace. Did you have a nice bath?" he asked.

"I did," I replied. "Are you having issues with the coffee pot?"

"No, it's fine," he said.

"Are you okay?" I asked. When I approached him, I felt his agitation.

"I'm fine," he repeated.

Walking up next to him, I put my back to the counter to watch the kids play. As I leaned up against it, he dared to look at me. I cut my eyes to him, waiting for him to give me a signal.

"She wants to get married as soon as possible," he said.

"And?"

"It's not a proper courtship," he said.

"Oh, really. How long should you court her before you get married?" I asked.

"It isn't a matter of time, but more of a mutual agreement of readiness," he said.

"Astor, she loves you. You love her," I said.

"I do," he said. "But it feels rushed."

"My advice is to not waste time. You never know how much time we have left," I said.

He refused to look at me because he knew that I knew exactly how that felt. I truly believed if he loved her, then they should make a go of it. The sooner the better. I didn't want him to make the same mistakes I had with Dylan thinking we had lifetimes to share each other.

"Thank you, Grace," he said quietly. "Be sure to heed your own words."

I lifted my eyes to meet Levi's. He winced, then looked away. "I'm not ready for different reasons," I said.

"Are they good enough reasons that if he perishes tomorrow you wouldn't regret it?" he said.

"If he perishes tomorrow, I will perish with him," I said.

"And your children?" he asked.

"I've made preparations," I said. While upstairs after my bath, I called my lawyer Remington Blake. Remy and Tabitha were preparing for their Samhain dinner. I gave him specific instructions related to my children and their care should something happen to me. I refused to let it happen though. I did the smart thing and planned ahead, but Levi and I would make it through this. I wasn't sure if we would lose anyone, but we would prepare for the worst. Hope for the luck that we needed to win.

"We better get moving," Levi said, calling my attention back to the tasks at hand.

"Yep, I'm ready," I said. Giving the kids hugs and kisses, we promised to return for Samhain dinner and the celebration.

We walked out the front door, heading toward the truck when he grabbed my hand. "Office."

The portal opened before us, and he dragged me through it into my office at the trailer.

"What are you doing?" I asked.

"We need to talk," he said.

"Levi, why do we have to have these conversations here?" I asked.

"Because you need to remember things sometimes, and I have to be the one to remind you. This place. This trailer is more like home to us than that house. I love the house. It's perfect for the kids, but this is us," he said.

"Not us," I said.

"Us."

"What the hell has gotten into you? You were listening to Astor," I said.

"I was," he huffed as he paced the room.

"Say what you have to say. We have work to do," I said, putting my hands on my hips.

"You could have just a little compassion for me in this situation," he said. I felt a full brooding fit coming on. I had compassion. I just had no idea what to do with it.

"What preparations did you make for the kids?" he asked.

"If something happens and we both don't come back, Astor and Ella are to take them. If they don't, then Tabitha and Remy will take them," I said. "I gave Remy access to some of the things I've stored up over the ages, and he will make sure that they get them when they get older. Was I supposed to get your permission or opinion on my children?"

"Why are you being hateful?" he asked.

"I don't know, Levi. You dragged me through a portal demanding to talk. So, get to the real reason we are here," I said.

"Fine," he said.

"I'm waiting," I replied.

He paced back and forth again. Then stopped in the middle of the floor. I felt him fighting for the right words to say when I knew there were only three that would make it okay. He wanted to explain. Preface it. However, he just needed to say it.

"Levi," I said.

"No, just give me a minute," he replied.

"Okay," I said, then leaned against the wall to wait on him.

The silence yawned between us. It was waiting too.

"I know that I have said it before, but I need to say it again," he said.

"You don't have to."

"Would you please just shut up for a minute?" he asked.

I bit my top lip and nodded.

"Thanks. Now I've got to work it up again. Stop throwing me off," he said. "I love you isn't enough. I've tried to think of a thousand ways to explain it to you, but I couldn't because you're hurting. I feel that pain and the last thing I ever want to do is add to it. You were right. There are things that should be said and not pushed aside while waiting for the perfect time. This is *so* not the perfect time, but it may be the only time I have."

He leaned back on the edge of the desk, then dared to look at me. Keeping my emotions in check proved to be harder than what I thought it would be. He took my silence as a go ahead. If it got too much, I would have to skip out on him. The last thing I wanted to do was run because he needed to get this off his chest. And because I had stopped running.

He stood up to face me. Whatever he had to say, he wanted to say it to my face. He took a few steps toward me, and I instinctively straightened. I didn't want him to touch me. Not right now with all the tension in the room.

"Just so you know, this has nothing to do with Dylan or his dream," he said.

"Okay," I whispered.

"The only way I know how to explain to you what happens to me when I'm with you is to put it into the terms that I understand the most. Through music," he said.

Dear goddess. If he started to sing, I was going to lose it.

"Your life is like a symphony, Grace, with different movements. Some parts of the piece are fast paced and light. Others are dark and low. All of those things make up who you are. It's how I see you. I can see the magic of music through my sight, but I see the music of you without it. The light. The dark. It's not that I love all of those parts; it's that my heart is tuned to all of it. It only plays the right notes when I'm with you. Everything I've done since I came home from the Otherworld was to make sure that I could play it perfectly for you. With you. But with this battle on the horizon, we haven't gotten to the movement where our hearts play together. So, we both have to survive this. My greatest composition will never be complete if we don't."

Holy fucking metaphor. At times, I was sure that my bard possessed an old soul. No one talked like that anymore, but I remembered a man who once did. Taliesin. I didn't know if it was a product of my father's gift to Levi or if he was already like that before it was given to him. All I knew was that he knew how to melt me with his sincerity.

I couldn't speak, and I didn't know how to respond. He waited patiently for me to make the next move. So, I did. Crossing the room, I wrapped my arms around his waist and laid my head on his chest. He hugged me back tightly as his heart pounded against my ear. He brushed his fingers lightly through the ends of my hair.

Stepping away from him, I leaned on the desk where he once was. I grabbed his hand, so he would move closer to me. His other hand found my neck sending chills through me.

"Levi, this story isn't over. Our story. It's just starting, but I can't rush this. There are days when I don't know which way is up. I just need time," I said.

"And if we don't have any more time?" he asked.

"Then you should know that I love you with all that I have left to love. It's just a drop in my rusted bucket though," I said.

"Best damn looking rusted bucket I've ever seen," he smiled.

"As we go through each and every day, you feel the emotions inside of me. I don't hide them," I said.

"You don't. You're a whirlwind right now. I get that, but all the talk back at the house about saying what needed to be said, I had to talk about it. Selfish of me. I'm sorry," he said.

"Don't be sorry, because I know you aren't. I'm not sorry you said it either. I'm just sorry I can't reciprocate. However, we are as tight as ever," I said. "We need to get moving though."

He leaned over like he was going to kiss me, but kissed my cheek instead. That spot on my cheek sent a chill through me. A wonderfully, cold chill. His emotions settled, and a sense of purpose returned to his eyes. "Yes, we've got a town to save."

"And a hunt to stop," I said.

CHAPTER TWENTY-FIVE

THE FLORAL UPHOLSTERY ON BETTY'S COUCH REMINDED ME OF A weaver that I met in Europe. He was from the Middle East and his designs popped off the fabric. Back then, I had purchased a light gauzy bolt that he had in his shop in Paris. I took it back to the traveling fairies to make skirts for the women.

"You've got to be kidding me," Betty said.

"Grace, I don't think they will agree," Luther added who seemed to be out of the bottle for now.

"I'm not. I think it will work. We need to hit them with all of our resources. We need to contact your friend, Rosty, and let him know we won't be needing his services. Levi will take care of his payment," I said. "Unless he wants to join the fight, then I'm happy to have him. I won't pay him extra."

"How are you going to pay him?" Luther asked.

"What do you mean?"

"His requirements are unusual," he said.

"They are, but Levi spoke with Tennyson, and the items have been brought in. We are storing them in the vault for the time being," I said.

"Tennyson does have his hand in everything," Luther said.

"That he does," I replied. "But I need a banshee. Unless you know of another here."

"I'm the only one," Betty said. "The consequences of this will go beyond this fight. Once people know what I am and what I do, things will change."

"Things are always changing. We will adapt. Hell, look at me. I've changed," I said.

Levi let out a grunt. I rolled my eyes, but Betty and Luther grinned.

"I'll do it," Betty said.

"Fan-fucking-tastic!" I said. "We will get out of your way. Happy Samhain. We will see you tomorrow afternoon in front of the Food Mart."

Leaning back in my chair, I tried to play it cool. It wasn't every day that you summoned a ghoul to visit. Even in Shady Grove, it was a bit unusual.

"He's coming," Levi said.

"Yep," I replied. I could feel his cold lurk moving on the outside of the trailer office.

He rose up out of the floor as before, but this time, the shapeless form looked extremely pissed off. His eyes glowed as he stared at me.

"Before you eat us all alive, I have a proposition for you," I said.

"I'm not making deals with a fairy!" he said.

"It is a dangerous thing to do, but please hear me out. Do you have a name?" I asked.

"Before this job, I was known as Edward," he said.

"Ah, Eddie," I said.

"Edward," he repeated.

"Eddie," I said with a wink. He huffed. I could charm a ghoul. Levi shook his head.

"Go ahead with your proposal, Queen," he said.

"I have spoken to the Banshee. She will resume her duties

tomorrow night on Samhain," I said. "I would like to invite you to the occasion."

"There is a catch," he said.

"There is. And because I'm a good little fairy, despite what they say about me, I'm going to tell you the whole story. When I'm done, I'm sure we can come to a mutual agreement," I said.

Levi and I explained to him the plan for tomorrow night's impending attack. Eddie seemed curious that I would offer a being like him such an opportunity, but he did not hesitate to agree under one condition.

"If the Banshee does not wail, we take her," he said.

I sighed. Betty had to keep her side of the bargain or I would have to go against my word to Eddie, the head ghoul. "Agreed," I said.

"*It will work out,*" Levi said.

"*I hope so. We are in deep shit on this one,*" I said.

Sipping on the coffee that Nestor provided, Levi and I talked to him about his role in the fight. He agreed that he would be most helpful for taking care of the children.

"I went to see her again," he announced after we told him the plan.

"And?" I replied.

"She is unrepentant. After talking to her for a while, I think you underestimate the ORCs," he said as he pulled up a stool next to me.

"I don't. Robin single-handedly turned my life upside down," I said. "I give her plenty of credit."

"They are not just coming for you, but for all of the Other-world. They want to see the balance overthrown. As much as I don't like the Summer Realm, it is equal to us. It must remain intact," he said.

"It needs a King," I said.

"I agree," he replied. "Someone who will stand with you."

"I'm already working on that," I said.

Nestor looked at Levi, who shrugged. "It's not me," Levi said.

"No, it's not," I said.

"Astor," Nestor guessed.

"Yes," I said. "He deserves it. He is a good man and loyal. Plus, he's in love. It won't be long, and he will have his own Queen."

"How do you plan to do it?" Nestor asked.

"I'm just trying to live through tomorrow. I have no idea," I said.

We sat in silence for a few minutes. The bar was empty. Most of the town's businesses were closed. We had spread the word earlier of the impending fight. Levi and I were waiting on the response of the townspeople to decide how big of a force we could count on to battle the Wild Hunt. Tennyson called earlier to confirm that Brockton and the others in the Otherworld were preparing to raise it. He assured me that we would be ready.

"Are the rumors true?" Nestor turned to Levi.

"What rumors?" Levi asked.

"That you have the Great Sword," he said.

"They are true," Levi responded.

"You gave it to him?" Nestor asked me.

"The Lady of the Lake gave him the opportunity, and the sword chose him," I said.

"It chose well," Nestor said.

"Thank you, Nestor," Levi said.

"We are celebrating tonight. Are you going to join us?" I asked.

"Of course. No need to be here alone," he said.

"You know, we have plenty of room at the house. You're welcome to move in with us," I said.

Nestor paused, then shook his head. "No, this is home for me. This is where I need to be," he said.

"The offer stands," I said.

"Thank you, Grace. I love ya," he said.

A large hand pounded on the door outside. Nestor had locked it since he was closed. He didn't want to have to run anyone out.

"I'll get it," Levi said.

He walked to the door, opening it to find Rostam Dastan at the door. "Is she here?" he asked.

Levi opened the door wider, and the rude man strutted inside.

"Who the hell do you think you are?" he shouted at me.

Levi lowered his head behind him, and I felt the power in the room rush to him. I gave him a warning look, then turned to the loud man.

"Mr. Dastan," I said.

"Prince Dastan," he corrected.

"Ah, yes. Prince. Which is lower than a Queen, so I suggest you show some respect. I thought we discussed this before," I said.

"I show respect where it is earned," he said. "How dare you try to get me to join your little war!"

"You may leave this town," I said. "Whether I pay you or not, I'll decide that based on how quickly you leave."

"You will pay me. We agreed!" he yelled.

"I paid you to do a job, which you did not do. I took care of it myself. Therefore, your services are no longer needed," I said.

"Fairy deals!" he squealed.

I stood up allowing the power of Winter to take over me. My black dress swirled around my legs and the blue filigree stretched across my chest. The room turned cold, and a light snow started to fall.

"I am Gloriana, daughter of Oberon, Queen of the Exiles. You're in my town and will abide by my law," I said.

He snarled looking at me. "You're nothing but a glorified trailer trash queen," he said.

"Why, thank you," I replied. "That's the nicest thing you've ever said to me."

His insult was a reminder to me of who I was. If I needed to throw down, I wasn't above playing dirty. Perhaps I'd start with the arrogant Prince Dastan.

"Pay me, so that I may leave this place before the hunt arrives. If you don't, I'll give your Uncle whatever he needs to bring you down," he demanded.

"You would only die in a confrontation with the Wild of the Otherworld. I understand that you need to run," I said.

"You cannot goad me into this," he said.

"No, of course not, but if you don't do as I have asked, I will make you," I said.

He laughed and it filled the room. "I'd like to see you try," he said.

I let the cold darkness of my soul fill my intentions. Levi watched me closely. He was my life preserver. He would stop me before I went too far.

"You might be feeling a little weak in the knees," I said.

Instead of stopping me, Levi joined in. A thrum of strings filled the room as a spell unleashed from his tattoo. Prince Dastan sank to his knees on the floor. I didn't have to do a damn thing.

I raised my eyebrows at Levi. Perhaps I was a bad influence. He tilted his head sideways as if he didn't care. It made me smile.

"I like you better silent, too," I said, reaching forward with my power. A collar of ice formed around his neck. He started to choke and wheeze. "That sounds brutal. What do you think, Levi?"

"Collars suck," Levi responded.

"Aw , poor Prince Dastan. You should have left when I asked you to leave. I have a thing about people who threaten me and my family," I said.

His eyes bulged out of his head as he turned purple from the collar up.

"Maybe you should let him go," Nestor suggested.

"Maybe. But something tells me he hasn't learned his lesson," I said. "Have you learned your lesson?"

Dastan nodded vehemently. I waved my hand releasing the collar. He sank to the floor holding his neck, gasping for air. Then, I made the move to give him the opportunity. Turning my back on him, I walked back to my coffee cup on the bar. I heard him shuffle to his feet and the dragging sound of metal on sheath as he drew his long sword. I did not turn, because I felt Levi's power move once again.

A hard thud followed by the clanging of sword on wood echoed through the icy bar. Looking over my shoulder, the Prince in all of his glory was silent at my feet. Levi stood next to him holding Excalibur by the blade.

"I never realized the hilt of that thing was so heavy," I said.

Levi held it toward me, and I took it from him. "It has to balance the blade," he explained.

"Interesting. Bet that leaves a knot," I said.

"I jerked a knot on his head," Levi said. Nestor laughed.

"Eh, that one was a miss," I said. Levi stuck his lip out in a pout. "What? It wasn't *that* funny!"

"Whatever. I'm hilarious. What are we going to do with him?" Levi asked.

"I'm thinking we should drag him outside of the ward and take his clothes," I said.

"Juvenile," Nestor said.

"Yes, but very trashy," I responded. "We will even give him his payment."

"Really?" Levi said.

"Yep," I replied.

Levi and I watched the naked Persian demigod curse us through the ward. He couldn't see us, but we could see him. He stomped back and forth across the pavement. His only adornment was his belt and sword. I felt he might need the sword at some point. The rest of his clothing would be returned to him via human mail. In his right hand, he held a purple felt whiskey bag that I took from Hot Tin Roof. Inside it held thirty pieces of gold Darics, the ancient coin of the Persian empire. Tennyson pulled some major strings to get the coinage in time to pay the pompous asshole.

After reading through Levi's information about Dastan, I had learned that he liked to play tricks. Levi and I had agreed that a trick needed to be played on him if he caused trouble. He was actually more like Odysseus than Achilles. A trick for the trickster. He got the trick and the treat, and he had better be damn glad that was all he got.

"From now on we handle our own shit," Levi said.

"I agree," I replied. "Although, this is too much fun."

"It's so bad," he said, but he laughed.

"Yes, it is," I replied.

"He's lucky I didn't kill him," Levi said.

"You wouldn't have," I said.

"I would have if he had laid a hand on you," he said.

"My knight in shining armor," I replied.

"I think it's about time that I get that armor you promised me back when the sylph was here," he said. I thought back to when I had gained the blessing of the first elemental stone. Finley was there in his armor. Dylan had shifted into a Native American warrior which I had to admit was pretty damn hot. But Levi had felt out of place. I did promise to get him some armor. I supposed I could come up with something for him on short notice.

"You're right. I owe you," I said.

"I like it when you're agreeable," he said as he backed up the truck to turn us around.

I took one last look at the man across the ward. We had probably just saved his life because tomorrow might be the last day that Shady Grove existed.

CHAPTER TWENTY-SIX

TENNYSON WAS BUSY PREPARING FOR WAR, SO WE SKIPPED THE planned meeting. He promised to catch Levi up on all his activities later in the evening. We gave him our news about Betty, Edward, and Dastan.

"Please tell me you took pictures," I heard Jenny say in the background.

"Video," Levi said.

"You didn't!" I gasped.

"You need to pay more attention to technology," he said.

"I didn't know what you were doing with that thing. It's a phone. Not a camera," I said.

Jenny laughed as Tennyson said goodbye.

Our Samhain celebration began at dusk. Our extended family joined us. William arrived first. Levi greeted him, treating him with more respect than I had ever seen him do. Perhaps that relationship would get better for the both of them.

Astor greeted Ella, Mayor Jenkins, and Chaz Leopold when they arrived. It was nice to have all of them there to remember our dead.

Nestor came in with several wine offerings. It reminded me of the first time he came to the trailer with the wine. It was the night he told me who he was. I was so thankful to have at least one member of my blood here to remember our past as well.

Levi and I had cleared the coffee table to create a shrine for the dead. Astor had prepared a meal for us all to share afterward. We all gathered with a candle to represent the ancestor that we were memorializing tonight.

Winnie insisted on showing her new skills. She walked very slowly to each candle, lighting them perfectly. I held my breath each time, hoping she wouldn't cause any major damage. She did a fantastic job, and I was very proud of her.

Levi started us off with a passage from a new songbook. His songbook.

"Goddess of the tree of Life, as the veil thins, send us our beloved dead so that we may remember and honor them. Horned god of the forest, protect us from the evil which will try to cross into our realm. Grant us the power to turn back those who would destroy us. As this new year begins, let us all be thankful and remember the past to make us strong. Bless us this coming year to bear the fruits of wisdom and joy," he said, then lowered his book. "Ella, you guys go first."

Ella walked forward to the table with Eugene and Chaz. "This is for my mother, Laudine. You're remembered and loved," she said, setting her candle on the table.

Astor sat his candle on the table and simply said, "For my wife in my past life, Condi."

Nestor was next with his candle. Setting it down, he bowed his head. "For my daughter, Ellessa." My mother, whom I only barely knew, had died when Brockton took the Otherworld. We suspected that he had killed most of my father's harem that refused to service him. He would pay for those deaths as well. One day. Hopefully soon.

Levi and William shared a candle. William looked grave but sober. "This light is for my mother who was a light to us. May we carry her love to those around us so that her light continues to shine."

Levi took Aydan from my arms as we walked up to join him. We held three candles. Winnie placed hers down and said as she had practiced, "This is for my mother, Bethany, who is up in heaven looking down on me." She sat the second candle down.

"This candle is for my father, Oberon, King of the Otherworld. His legend lives in the hearts and souls of all that knew him. May his kingdom continue on for many years to come," I said.

I sat the candle in my hand on the table. Winnie said, "This is for my daddy, Dylan, who gave me his power and saved my life. I love you, Daddy."

"Dylan, my love, we go forward from this day with your spirit in our hearts. I will honor your memory and our love until the last day that I draw breath. I miss you so much." I wrapped my arm around Levi's and leaned on him. "Thank you for the gift to our daughter and for this beautiful boy, our son."

"We invite these honored dead to join us in a silent meal. We have a plate at the table in your memory," Levi said.

I bent down to wipe Winnie's tears. "You okay, baby?" I asked her.

"Yeah, I just miss him," she said.

"Me too," I said.

"He would have liked this," she said.

"Yes, he liked to celebrate holidays," I replied.

"We have to be quiet at dinner?" she asked.

"Yes," I said. I didn't think we could be quiet for the entire dinner, but we were going to try for tradition's sake.

We each took our places, and at one end of the table a chair was draped with a black cloth. This was our spirit chair. The reserved place for those who had gone on into the next life.

Surprisingly, the only one to make noise during the dinner was Aydan and we figured he would get a pass. Although at one point he realized he was the only one making noise, and he got louder and louder. Winnie giggled at him, but that was the extent of the noise outside of plates and utensils being passed around.

Astor and Ella cleared the table, and each one of us left the room by stopping at the Spirit Chair to thank our ancestors for joining us. I was the last one to leave.

"I love you. Thank you for loving me back," I said, then turned off the light.

"Phew, I'm glad that is over," Winnie exclaimed. "I thought this was supposed to be fun."

"Now is the fun part," I said.

Levi came out of the kitchen with a pumpkin. "Let's carve this!" he announced.

Winnie jumped up and down clapping. Aydan joined in the clapping with no idea what was going on. Astor served desserts with all sorts of pumpkin themes, but we also had apple tarts which were the traditional fruit of Samhain.

After the pumpkin carving, we said goodbye to our guests except for Nestor and William. Astor drove Ella home. He told me not to expect him back tonight. I didn't comment, even though I wanted to.

"Thank you for joining us, William," I said.

"Thank you for having me, Grace. It was a nice dinner. I believe our dead would have been proud," he said. "I wish there was something I could do to help with this battle ahead."

"You can stay out of it," Levi said. "I don't want you dead, Father."

"Perhaps I can help with the children," he offered.

"I think that will be a good idea," I said. "Meet up at the vault tomorrow afternoon."

"I am going to head home. Goodnight, everyone," he said.

"Night, Mr. William," Winnie said. He smiled and waved at her as he left.

Levi sat down next to me after seeing his father to the door. He propped his legs up on the coffee table.

"Get your feet down from there," Winnie said.

"Wynonna Riggs, what has gotten into you?" I asked.

"Feet don't belong on the table," she said smartly.

"You better change your tone or you're going to bed," I said.

"Grace, it's okay," Levi said putting his hand on my thigh. He removed his feet from the table.

"Say you're sorry, Winnie," I said.

"No," she said.

"Young lady, what has gotten into you?" I asked.

"If you hadn't been a Queen, then Daddy would still be here. The kids at school say it all the time. It's your fault he died. He's not here because of you! I'm not doing what you tell me to do anymore," she screamed at me. She threw her hands out toward me, as fire erupted from them across the room. Levi couldn't move fast enough to block the fireball. It hit the couch and our clothes, starting small fires. Levi and I frantically patted the fires on each other then on the couch.

My winter power had kept us from being burned when I swung around to face Winnie she stood with her hands in front of her gaping mouth.

"Winnie," I whimpered. Her words cut through me again and again. If Dylan hadn't fallen in love with me, he would be alive. Even if he had stayed with Stephanie, I don't think she would have ever killed him or caused him to die. Winnie was right. It had been there in the back of my mind all of this time.

"Momma," she muttered.

"Grace, don't," Levi said. "Winnie, go up to your room."

"Momma, I'm sorry," she said, then took off in a full sprint up the stairs.

"Grace, she is a child. Kids say things they don't understand," he said.

"She understood. She's right," I said, looking at the burn marks on the couch.

"No, Grace, she's not. You know that," Levi said.

"If he didn't love me, he would be alive," I said.

Nestor stood across the room stunned by the exchange.

"Nestor, will you go check on Winnie?" Levi asked.

"Yeah, sure," he said, then hurried up the steps to Winnie's room.

My body shook with the grief and pain of my child's words. I swayed losing control of the despair that I had locked inside. Levi jumped up in front of me, grabbing my face.

"Look at me, Gracie," he said. "Come on, if it's got to be now, so be it. Let it out."

I shook my head, but my chest hurt with the strain. "No. The fight is tomorrow," I said.

He pulled me tighter to him, even though I pushed away. These were the moments when I remembered that Levi had a lot more strength than it looked like. "We aren't doing anything else until you scream and cry. I'm not letting you go," he said.

"Let go of me!" I demanded.

"No," he said defiantly.

"Levi, I swear. I am not playing with you!" I said.

"Don't care. I'm not letting go," he said.

"You were in the Otherworld with him. You should have told me what was going on. I could have gotten to him. I could have stopped this!" I screamed.

"Yes, I was there. I made the best decision I could. I did what he asked me to do," he said.

"Let go! I don't want you touching me!" I yelled, pushing against his chest.

"It's my fault, too. Just like it's yours. It's Stephanie's fault. It's Robin's fault," he said, pushing my emotions to the edge.

"Yes! It is!" I pounded on his chest, but he didn't budge.

"Hit me harder, Grace. Let me have it," he said as tears formed in the edges of his eyes. His sad cobalt eyes.

Anguish ripped me into shreds as I watched him cry for me. My knees buckled and his grip went from containment to support. Excruciating sorrow vibrated through my body into his. The tingle between us was an aching throb of heated pain.

The sob started in the back of my throat but caught in my mouth like I was choking. Levi eased us to the floor where I grasped at his shirt for support. He leaned back against the couch, and I practically crawled into his lap. The tears escaped my eyes with abandon. There was no stopping it now. Wet spots formed on his shirt from the downpour of emotion from my eyes.

I relived his final moments, over and over in my head trying to figure out a way I could have stopped it, but there was nothing. Each time the scene ended the same.

Dylan dead.

Winnie changed.

I broke.

I felt like I was going mad. One minute I was living life, taking care of my children. I got lost in my duties as Queen only to find no completion in it. Jokes weren't funny like they used to be. Happiness was hollow and short. The next minute, something would trigger a memory that I would have to tuck away because of the pain.

I just didn't want to feel like this anymore.

"Make it stop," I begged to no one in particular.

"This agony is the darker part of love. But you can find peace in that it was true. So true that the absence of it can bring you to your knees," Levi said.

Love so deep that it bore a hole like a cold well in my body. Now it was an empty, dark cavern. The reason I couldn't love Levi was that there was no way he could ever fill that void. Panic set in, and I pushed away from him again.

"No, don't," he said, tightening.

"You want me to have another hole in my heart. One for you. So, when something happens to you, I'll be completely and utterly destroyed?" I asked.

He held me with one arm around my waist but freed the other hand to brush down my cheek. "You're too strong to be destroyed," he said.

"Yeah, look at me, a whimpering baby," I said.

"All I see is a woman who loved more than she ever thought possible," he said.

"You think that comforting me is going to secure your place?" I lashed out at him.

He took it in stride. He had pushed me to it, and now he had to accept the wrath that came with it. "If you're truly honest with yourself, Grace, you know that I already have a place there. Part of this pain is guilt. I feel it too. I loved him, but I love you more than anything in this world. For me to ever have what I wanted, he would have to make a huge mistake or die. I knew those things would hurt you more than I was willing to gamble. I did everything I could to keep him alive for you."

"I'm not guilty. We haven't done anything," I protested.

"Lie to no one else, Miss Fairy, but go ahead lie to yourself," he said. "We haven't done anything, but you feel guilty anyway because of what you feel. Even if it isn't acted upon."

Finally, he let go, and I sat up to look at him. "What do we do? Tell me what to do," I said.

"What would he want you to do?" he asked.

"Go kick ass," I said.

"So, we go kick ass," he said.

"Winnie," I muttered. "What a mess."

The consequences of not facing this pain boiled down to the point where my child needed me and her hurtful words came from a place in her heart that ached too. I wasn't able to be strong enough for her when she needed.

"Go talk to her," Levi said.

I wiped the tears from my cheeks with the palms of my hands. Just before I got up, I looked down into Levi's still saddened eyes. He still had a spark of life and hope there. I put my hands on his cheeks like he had done to me, pulling his forehead to mine. He was right. There was a big chunk of my heart that belonged to my bard.

"You," I said, getting choked up again. "It isn't attractive to be right all the time."

"I'll keep that in mind," he said with a sideways grin.

"Thank you, Dublin," I said.

He sucked in a deep breath, restraining himself. He took one of my hands from his cheek, then kissed my palm. "Go see Winnie," he whispered.

"Okay," I replied. He helped steady me, as I stood, then when I gained my balance, I ran up the stairs after my daughter.

LEVI

FOR MONTHS, I WATCHED HER WALK-THROUGH LIFE AS AN EMPTY shell. The hole in Grace's heart ate away at every part of her. She didn't cuss as much, which wasn't so bad, but it was a clear indication that she wasn't fine as she claimed to be.

Other people had noticed, but no one could feel her like me. The vibrant life she once lived was replaced by an empty cavern. She blamed herself. She blamed me. She teetered back and forth between faux anger and faux happiness.

Dylan died, but Grace was the ghost. A haunting of what she had once been. Each day she tucked away the grief. Sure, she cried in the dark. She held on to the leather jacket. But she never let herself just weep.

I knew that if she was ever to truly live again, she needed to mourn Dylan. Not just have a good, ugly cry. She needed to blame herself and me. She needed to scream and get angry. She needed to fight back at death.

Closer and closer, she moved to that breaking point. I felt it shatter inside of her when Winnie screamed at her. Those childish words became the catalyst to force Grace to face the emotions swirling inside of her.

When she hit me, it felt good. I hurt for him and her both, but to see her finally lash out, to overreact, I knew she would make it out of this fog. I didn't care if she hit me a hundred times. I would have taken every blow with pride.

What I wasn't prepared for was her to admit that I was right. That she felt guilty because she did have feelings for me. I couldn't get her off my lap fast enough. Grace was still stubborn, but there were things now that she was willing to concede. So many times, in the last few months, she admitted she was wrong. She let someone else lead the way. It was a change in her character that made her even more beautiful to me. I loved the sassy fairy in her, but this humble heart had me reeling.

I just hoped that once she spoke to Winnie that the two of them could reach an understanding. Back when Winnie was dead on that field, I thought it impossible to change her to a fairy. The criteria demanded that the recipient of the fruit and water be enthralled. Grace realized what I didn't. Winnie was utterly in love with Dylan. The father she had never had.

I knew that feeling. It didn't matter that Grace and I shared the blood oath. I was completely and hopelessly enthralled to the point where my heart didn't matter. I just wanted hers to be whole again. Admitting to me that I held a part of it completed my life in a way I hadn't expected. If nothing else ever happened between us, I knew that a piece of her heart belonged to me, and it was enough.

∼

Nestor joined me in the hallway as Winnie and Grace talked out what happened. Winnie cried and held on to her mother's neck. They both said they were sorry. Winnie insisted that Grace read her a bedtime story, and of course, she picked one of the ones that Dylan loved the most. Grace read through the story with a strong voice.

I felt the strength growing inside of her. I was so thankful. I had concluded that if she didn't let go at some point before the battle with the hunt that I would have to knock her out and hide her away. I feared that she might get distracted or apathy would kick in at the wrong time.

"What you did for her down there, what you have been doing, I am so grateful, Levi. No one could bring her out of this except you," Nestor said.

"She did most of it. I just needed to be there when she finally decided to accept the emotions," I said.

"Forgive me for ever doubting how much you love her," Nestor said.

I twisted my head to look at him. "You doubted it?" I asked.

"Yes. You're young, Levi. I didn't know if this was just a simple crush or the real thing," he said.

"It's been a real thing since the first time I laid eyes on her.

Crush, maybe. Hopeless, definitely," I said. "Even if nothing ever becomes of us, I'm happy to know that she can feel joy again."

"Like you said, forgive me for listening in, you already have a place in her heart. She just has to get used to the idea of how that fits along with the missing pieces," Nestor said. "I have confidence that the two of you will figure it out. In the meantime, I ask you not to manhandle my granddaughter again."

"Yes, sir," I muttered.

"Good job, Son," he said. "See you tomorrow."

Nestor walked down the steps and out the front door, leaving me alone with Grace and the kids. I heard her finish up the story with Winnie, and they shared many goodnight hugs and kisses.

"Uncle Levi," Winnie called out to me.

I stuck my head in the door, "Yeah?"

"I love you, Uncle Levi," she said. "I'm sorry I tried to burn you."

"I love you, too, Winnie," I said.

"Night, Momma," she said. Grace kissed her on the forehead, then met me in the hallway.

"Momma," a little voice said.

Grace looked back at Winnie, but we both knew it wasn't her.

"Momma," it said again.

"Oh, my goddess," she gasped, running down the hall to Aydan's room. I ran behind her, and when she turned on the light, he was standing in the crib. "Aydan?"

"Momma," he said lifting his arms to her.

He had better timing than I did.

She rushed to pick him up, squeezing him tightly. He hugged her back, then smiled at her.

"You're supposed to be asleep," she said to him.

"Momma!" he exclaimed.

She looked at me in wonder. I felt her heart thumping with love for this child. I knew inside of her, that she loved Aydan, but he was a constant reminder of what she had lost. But now, he was a reminder of what she had gained. A new outlook. A hope for the future.

"Alright! Alright! Time to lay down," she said. "Levi, get the light please."

I flicked the switch and watched her coax Aydan back to sleep. Looking at her through my sight, she glowed a pale blue. Her light had almost gone out, but I didn't have the heart to tell her. Now I saw that illumination and knew she would make it through this.

CHAPTER TWENTY-EIGHT

GRACE

ONE LITTLE WORD AND MY HEART SURGED TO BEAT AGAIN AFTER THE numb feeling had replaced my despair. When I stepped out of Aydan's room, Levi waited on me with a huge grin on his face.

"He said it," I whispered.

"Yes, he did," he said.

"I thought he would never," I said.

"He has good timing. I have to admire that," Levi said.

"He must have learned that from you," I replied. "Why are you looking at me like that? Are you using your sight?"

"Yeah," he said, then looked at his feet. "Your light has changed."

"How?" I asked.

"It was fading. I'm sorry I've been a dick, but I've been worried," he said.

"And now it's better?" I asked.

"A little," he said. "It will take time. But, I won't be holding you down anymore."

"Huh?"

"Your Kelpie Grandfather threatened me," he said.

I laughed, but then covered my mouth because it was so loud. I hugged him.

"*As always, you did exactly what I needed you to do,*" I said.

"*Do you think you can sleep? You really need to rest before tomorrow. I'm afraid of how much power it's going to take for both of us,*" he said.

"*I think I can. Maybe,*" I replied.

It was a nice long hug. One that just a few hours ago I would have shied away from, but I needed to face the facts that just because Dylan was gone and left a hole in my heart, that my heart could love Levi, too. What that meant for our relationship, I wasn't even ready to start thinking about it. I needed to focus on the battle ahead for all the right reasons.

Vengeance for Dylan was one thing, but the provision of a future haven for our children was more important. I'd be damned if I was going to let Brockton and his Wild Hunt march in here and destroy this town.

"It's a little brighter," Levi said.

"Yeah, it is," I said. "Goodnight, Dublin."

"Night, Grace," he said as he backed into his room.

I curled up in my bed, and for the first time in a very long time, I slept.

When I woke up, two shining blue eyes stared at me from the side of the bed.

"Momma!" Aydan said.

"What are you doing?" I asked, reaching over to pull him up on the bed. He laughed and giggled as I tickled him. "Did you climb out of your bed? Levi!"

My shirtless bard showed up at the door. "How'd he get in here?" he asked as he approached the bed. He flopped down on the end of it bouncing Aydan and me up and down.

"I guess he finally climbed out. We've got to get a baby gate so he doesn't go down those steps," I said.

"I'll get one," Levi said. "You little stinker!" Levi grabbed him up and threw him in the air above the bed. Aydan laughed so loud that it woke his sister up.

"I want to play too," Winnie said.

"If you come over here, we will tickle you," I said.

"No!" she exclaimed, but ran and jumped on the bed with us. Levi handed me Aydan as he grabbed Winnie.

"Hold up there, Little Girl. I've got ya!" he said. She squealed.

"Uncle Levi! Have mercy! Mercy!" she yelled.

"No mercy for you!" he laughed in the worst evil laugh I'd ever heard.

"Tickle Momma!" Winnie said.

"No!" I exclaimed. "Levi Rearden!"

"Say his middle name, Momma. Like you do when you're mad," Winnie taunted.

"I don't know his middle name," I said.

"Oh, I do! It's…" she tried to speak, but Levi clamped his hand down on her mouth.

"My daughter knows and I don't!"

"She asked. I told her," he said. "Winnie, that's our secret. You can't tell your Momma."

"Don't make her keep secrets from me!" I protested.

He laughed releasing her mouth. "Ha! Ha! I know and you don't!"

"I'm gonna whip you both!" I said.

"No!" Winnie exclaimed.

"*Please*," Levi begged.

"Get out of this bed," I said shoving him with my feet.

"Stop kicking me," he whined.

"Alright. Everybody out. Let's go downstairs and get some breakfast," I ordered.

Winnie jumped off the bed and ran down the hallway. Her heavy feet pounded the floor until she got to the steps. They slowed for the descent, but not by much.

"You sure you want me out of the bed?" Levi said.

"Yes," I replied.

"You can't lie," he said.

"There are conditions on the statement," I said.

"What conditions?" he asked.

"Unspoken ones," I replied.

"Give me an example," he pressed.

"Like, for now," I said.

"See! I knew that aura boost was a little bit of hope," he grinned. "Come on, Little Bird. Those of us menfolk gotta get out of the lady's bed." Aydan reached up for him. One thing was for sure. Aydan wanted to be held by whoever was standing up if he had a choice.

After breakfast, we packed bags for the kids. Winnie wore an angel costume. I wasn't sure why she picked that one, but she had. At one time it fit her perfectly, but she was growing up. Forming her own opinions of the world. I just hoped that Levi and I could guide her in the right direction. It wasn't going to be easy with either one of them. I was just thankful that I had help.

CHAPTER TWENTY-NINE

We had one stop on our way to the Food Mart to meet up with everyone. There was a chill in the air along with heavy cloud cover. I hoped it wouldn't rain. It was bad enough we were going to have to fight, but I hated the rain. Snow, on the other hand, might be nice.

Levi pulled the truck up into the field where Ford and Wendy's band of traveling fairies lived. The bright RVs were arranged in a large circle with a couple of them in the middle. The children ran and played. All of them were dressed up for the holiday.

"I'll be just a minute," I said.

"Sure," Levi replied.

Ford had sent word that the gypsies were going to huddle up and protect their own. It was a typical response for them. I had traveled with them in Europe, and I knew all too well that we could only trust our own. I wanted to point out to Ford that I was one of them at one point. That they were a part of this community now. I didn't expect to persuade him, but I wanted to make my plea.

"Grace!" Wendy called out to me with a wave.

"Howdy," I said. "Is Ford around?"

"He is, but he said he didn't want to talk to you if you showed up," she said.

"Coward," I joked.

"He knew that you could be very persuasive. You should know this wasn't his decision alone. It was the decision of our whole group," she said.

"Ah! I see. There are no hard feelings. I thought I'd just give it a try," I said.

"For the record, I'm on your side," she said.

"What?"

"I think we should fight," she said. "If that hunt gets through you guys, it will run us over. I don't think we have enough magic to hold it back. Better that we stand in the front than die in the back."

"Thank you, Wendy," I said. It disappointed me that they didn't want to fight, but I understood it also. However, Wendy was right. If we failed at the front, there would be no stopping the hunt.

"Blessings and well wishes," she said.

"To you and yours, as well," I responded. "Happy Samhain."

Trudging back to the truck, I hoped that the rest of the town didn't take the position of the gypsies. If they did, we would be doomed.

The parking lot at the Food Mart was empty except for a few cars in front of Mike's Magic Vape Shop. We pulled up to the brightly sparkling building. Even without the sun, it was an impressive sight. We unloaded the kids and went inside.

"Afternoon, my Queen," Mike greeted me. "Miss Jenkins, Nestor, and the others are down in the vault."

"Afternoon and Happy Samhain," I said.

"Well, I suppose we will find out how happy it is shortly," he said.

"Indeed," I replied. Winnie was already pulling me down the steps to the vault. She gushed over the jeweled walls and the glittering portal.

When we stepped inside, we found more than just Ella and Nestor. Tennyson, Jenny, Troy, Amanda, Luther, Betty, and William were all there. In the center of the room, a set of armor glistened under a spotlight. It helped to have a blacksmith in town that knew the old ways. He apparently was a wonderful leatherworker as well.

Levi stared at the armor. I took Aydan from him so that he could look at it more closely. Each one of the knights wore similar armor, but Levi's had its own distinctions. The breastplate featured the same artwork as his original tattoo. The Celtic knotwork with the triquetra center. Embedded in the leather were emeralds like the ones on his tattoo. Each piece of leather featured knotwork. The bracers had triquetras in blue with silver snowflakes intertwined with musical notes. In fact, the entire set featured blue and silver.

"This is amazing," Levi said. "Thank you to whoever did this."

"It was Grace," Tennyson said.

"I didn't make it. I just had it made for you," I said. "I promised."

"You did. I thought you forgot," he said.

"Let's get you in this," Astor said.

Jenny and Ella took the kids upstairs. I followed them up. Mike made up some candy corn vape liquids. He had it burning in an incense pot. The kids exchanged candy and admired each other's costumes.

"Send him to the bar when he is ready," I said to Jenny.

"Sure thing," she said. "Good luck, Grace."

"Thanks," I said. She reached out and hugged me.

"You seem different today," she said.

"I am different," I replied. "I'll tell you about it when this is over."

"I look forward to it," she said.

I stalked across the empty parking lot. Reaching out with my senses, I felt the people of Shady Grove preparing for war. We would have a turnout. I just hoped it was enough.

Nestor left Hot Tin open for me. I slipped inside to psyche myself up for what I was about to do. Pulling the velvet box out of my pocket, I sat it on the bar next to a shot glass and a plate.

Closing my eyes, I concentrated on my personal armor. It looked very much like Levi's, but more feminine. Pulling on the magic of the Otherworld, my armor appeared on my body much as it had when I fought the sylph. However, the hunt's power exceeded that being by one-hundred-fold. It would take more than just fancy armor to beat it.

After what seemed to be a long wait in the dark, Levi appeared at the door in his armor. Excalibur hung by his side.

"Grace, what's going on?" he asked in the darkness of the bar. When the door shut behind him, my tattoo ignited sending the strands of blue hue around my body. The light was powerful enough to light up the room.

"We need to talk about a last few items before this battle," I said.

"You're blocking me," he said.

"I am, but for only a moment. I needed to collect my thoughts," I explained.

"Well, let's get on with it. I don't think we have much time," he said. I felt his nerves, his anxiety, but also his resolve. Sometimes fear and resolve were more powerful than confidence and bravery.

My heart pounded for what I was about to do, but I felt like in order to protect him, it needed to be done.

"Two things," I said.

"One," he said.

"One," I said handing him the velvet box.

"What's this?" he asked as he opened the box. Inside the bright cushion diamond flickered with blue light. "Is this the ring I gave you? Well, that your father gave me to give to you?"

"Yes," I said. "There is power in this ring. It was there once before when we pretended to be engaged. It helped you bring me back from the edge. I think that I need to wear it again. I don't want to go too far."

"You won't, and I don't need a ring to do that," he said.

"It also protects you, Levi. When we walk out of here, those who have chosen to fight with us will be out there. They need to see us as a cohesive unit," I said.

"A couple," he clarified.

"Yes, because they need to know they aren't being lead by a..."

"Bard," he smiled.

"Yeah, by a bard," I said.

"You're leading them. I'm just window dressing," he said.

"That sword is the sword of a king," I said.

"Grace," he started.

"Nope. Let me finish this," I said pausing. "I have said and will continue to say that we are solid. I have no doubts about our connection. I trust you more than anyone in this town. This is an outward display of that. It will give them the confidence to follow us both. If you give the order, it will be like it came from me."

"Then I should be wearing your ring," he said.

"It's the same difference," I said. "Plus, as much as I planned ahead, I didn't plan to get you a ring."

"How thoughtless of you," he said deflecting his fear in humor.

"Will you let me wear it again?" I asked.

"They will think we are engaged," he said.

"Are we engaged?" I asked lifting an eyebrow to see if he caught what I was saying.

"No more than the last time," he said.

"And yet, it still worked," I said.

He huffed. My romantic bard had other plans for giving me a ring one day, but this wasn't about that, and I needed to make sure we were clear on it.

"Alright," he said, handing me the ring. "Do you want me to kneel again?"

"No, silly," I said, taking the ring from him. But he held on to it, sliding it onto my finger himself.

"I think we discussed sexual privileges the last time you took this ring from me," he said.

"Yep, the answer is the same now as it was then," I grinned. He laughed.

"Can't blame a guy for trying. Okay, what's two?" he asked.

I walked over to the bar, and the blue light illuminated a shot glass with a blue liquid and a small plate with a piece of fruit.

"I'm already fairy," he said.

"Half," I replied.

"This works for humans," he said.

"I'm the queen, and I say it works for Changelings too," I replied.

"Why?" he asked.

"It is up to you. I'm offering, but please hear my reasoning," I requested.

"Go ahead," he said. Not like he would refuse me.

"As half-human, you're more vulnerable to fatal wounds. If you're a fairy, you will heal faster and the chances of you dying are a lot less," I said.

"I'm not going to die, Grace," he said.

"I want to make sure of it," I replied as tears welled up in my eyes. "I will not let them take someone else from me. Not ever again. I don't care what it takes. I will protect the people that I love!"

"This will change me," he said. "I might not be the same man you love."

"You will always be my Levi," I said. "Even if I don't know your middle name."

He laughed and kissed my cheek. "What if I'm like an ogre or something?"

"You can have the ring back," I teased.

"Oh! You're awful!" he said.

"I know," I replied. "Besides ogres and fairies aren't compatible."

"Huh?"

"Let's not talk about ogre anatomy," I said.

"Maybe later," he said.

"Later," I agreed.

Levi looked down at the water and fruit, then back at me. I could tell that he was afraid it would change who he was on the inside, but I knew that he was pure of heart. Nothing could ever change that.

As he reached for the glass, the room filled with light, blinding us both. Levi twisted around pulling the sword out which sang in his hand.

"Do not fear," a female voice said. "It is I, Lilith."

Her bright light toned down, and we gazed upon her pregnant beauty. Her large belly bulged as she smiled at us.

"Why are you here?" I asked.

"Because you're about to alter his life," she said. "You have already saddled him with the Great Sword and the responsibilities of a king."

"Yes, but this will protect him. Help keep him alive to do these things," I said.

"Perhaps your focus should be on those people out there and those below accepting him," she said. "Not on what *you* gain from it. Levi, you should make your decision on what you want to do. Don't do it because Grace is afraid to lose someone else she cares deeply for. Do it because it is something you want to do. Carry that sword because it is something that you feel compelled to do it. I know that she influences you very easily. Do not let her influence you on this point."

"I can't just walk away," he said.

"Sure, you can," she replied.

"No, a lesser man might, but not me," he said.

"Levi, you're still young. Grace has been on this earth for hundreds of years," she said.

"Thanks for pointing out how old I am," I said.

"This isn't about you," Lilith said.

I threw my hands up, moving away from them both. Was I being selfish asking Levi to do all of these things? I didn't want him to die. I couldn't take it. It was self-preservation. It was selfish. I turned back around.

"She's right," I said.

"What?" he said turning to me. "What do you mean?"

"It is selfish of me. I should have asked you if you wanted the sword instead of manipulating my way. I should have asked you to join this fight as a leader. And I do want you to take the drink and fruit so I don't lose you too," I said. "I'm sorry. You do what you want to do, Levi. Not what I want."

"If you haven't noticed, I chose to do all of this stuff around town without you," he said.

"For me," I said.

"So damn arrogant," he exclaimed. "Maybe for once, after seeing the evil that is your Uncle, I thought I should come back here and act like an adult. Take on responsibilities. Not just taking care of you and the kids, but being a help to our friends here. I did that for *me*!"

Lilith smiled as if she enjoyed him berating me. I wasn't a victim. For all my years, I was learning that even though I didn't grow up in my father's house that I was still a spoiled brat. I squeezed my eyes shut trying to block it out. We had the battle to fight, and this wasn't helping. His forehead touched mine, and his hands slid around my neck.

"I'm sorry," I muttered.

"I love your arrogant self," he said.

"I'm going to be better," I said.

"You already are," he whispered.

"It's interesting," Lilith said spoiling the private moment.

"Look, Josey," I said.

"Grace," Levi warned. I clamped my mouth shut.

"Levi, what was your mother's maiden name?" she asked.

"O'Sheen," he said.

"O'Sheen!" I exclaimed. "As in the Irish O'Sheens?"

He shrugged, "I guess."

I backed away from him, then looked to her. "No," I said.

"Yep," she said.

"Who are they?" he asked.

"Google it," I snapped.

"Little late for that," he said.

"The O'Sheens descend from Oisín," I said.

"Ireland's bard," he said.

"Exactly!" I said.

"He comes by it naturally," she smiled.

"Then what did my father give him?" I asked.

"An accelerated course," she said. "Essentially, he gave Levi a helpin' of bard with a songbook on the side."

"He knew," I said.

"Yep," she said quite satisfied with herself.

"What?" Levi asked.

"Oisín was the son of Fionn Mac Cuhaill and Sadhbh who was the daughter of Bodb Dearg!" I said.

"Your genealogy is impressive, Grace," she said.

"Thanks," I muttered. It was something we were made to learn under my father's orders.

"Piece it together for me," he said.

"Bodb Dearg was the heir to the Dagda," I said.

"THE Dagda?" Levi asked.

"Yes," I said. "You have royal blood. Royal fairy blood. Plus, Oisín was a deer like my father."

"He was?"

"Yes, his mother was changed into a deer, and he was born of her that way, but was able to change. He was a warrior and a poet," I explained.

"So, if I drink the water and eat the fruit, I'll more than likely be a stag," he said.

"Maybe," Lilith said. "Oh, I need to get going. I want to get a good seat for the fight."

"Are you hormonal? Pregnant women get hormonal and do weird things," I said.

"Probably," she smiled. "Y'all have fun."

Just like that, she was gone.

Levi didn't hesitate. He walked over to the water and fruit, shooting the water down and swallowing the fruit. He sank to a knee, grasping his throat.

"Shit! By the Queen of Winter and the King of Summer, I call upon thee, fairy child, rise!" I said almost forgetting my part in the change. He stood up nonchalant and winked at me. "Motherfucker," I said.

"Not yet, but are you volunteering?" he smiled.

"Feel different?" I asked, ignoring the innuendo.

"Nope," he said. "Alright, is that it?"

"No, but I'll tell you the rest later," I said.

"What?"

"Tell me your middle name," I said.

"No," he replied.

"Fine," I said.

"Fine," he copied. He held his arm up for me to take it. I snaked my arm through his, and he walked us out in the twilight. The parking lot was filled with the citizens of Shady Grove who all took a knee at our appearance. "Holy crap."

CHAPTER THIRTY

HE DROPPED HIS ARM, THREADING HIS FINGERS THROUGH MINE. I felt his heart racing. He wasn't used to this kind of attention.

"It's okay," I said. "This is what happens when you take a sword like Excalibur."

"Can I go back in the bar and take a few shots?" he asked.

"No," I laughed. I waved my hand trying to get everyone to stand.

Our friends and family stood around us. I paused for a moment to see if he would take over, and to my surprise, he did.

"Thank you all for coming today. We will show them what Shady Grove is about and that they aren't welcome here," he said as a cheer erupted from the group. "Tennyson, Troy, Astor, and Finley will divide you into groups. Grace and I will wait for their appearance. Each one of the knights will assign you an area to cover. Please keep in mind that our families are near, and those who couldn't fight. We stand for them too."

The knights began to direct traffic. Astor and Finley took a group of people into the Food Mart, while Tennyson and Troy took the rest into Hot Tin.

"Where is Luther?" I asked.

"Haven't seen him," Tennyson said as he directed traffic.

"Shit," I said looking to the sky for the Ifrit. "If she backs out on us, this might not work."

Levi squeezed my hand. "She will be here."

Tabitha approached with Remy. She handed me a long black cloak like the one I used to wear to hide my fairy form. It was a prop for today because I no longer had to hide who I was. "We are in Astor's group," she said.

"Are you fighting?" I asked.

She pulled a long-curved blade from a sheath on her back. "Yep. I'm a doctor. I know a few things about knives," she smiled.

"Nice," Levi said.

"We've got your back," Remy said. "Let's take it to them."

I nodded as they walked off to join Astor's group. Looking toward the Food Mart, I saw Finley. He blocked the woman that he was kissing, but when he moved away, she was unmistakable with her auburn hair.

"Riley," I snarled.

"Nothing we can do about that now," Levi said.

She saw us staring at her, and she dipped her head. Finley noticed and ran over to us.

"I should have told you we were together, but I knew you would flip out. I promise. I've been keeping an eye on her," Finley said.

I seethed on the inside. She had just been at my house and after Levi. Finley was thinking with his dick again.

"We will discuss it later," Levi said trying to avert my anger.

Finley looked to me for my response. This was the impulsiveness that I needed to control. "Later," I echoed Levi.

Finley nodded then ran back over to Riley who kissed him on the cheek, then loaded up in a car with Kadence Rayburn. They drove off without looking at us.

"The ex-girlfriend brigade. Nice," Levi said. "There is more to this."

"Is there?" I asked.

"Yes. I just don't know what," he said, watching them as they drove by.

Tennyson approached us.

"Everything is ready. Luther and Betty are on the way. Our dark friends are waiting below," he said.

"Thank you, Tennyson," I said.

"It is my pleasure to serve your family again," he said. "I can't thank you enough for what you've done for me."

"I'm really glad we got over that first encounter," I said.

"Grace, you come off as brash and irreverent, but most of us know your heart. That's what matters," he said. "Levi, you look good in armor. Don't get killed."

"That's the plan," Levi said.

"Grace, you still have that horse thing covered?" Tennyson asked.

"Yes," I replied.

"Horse thing?" Levi asked.

Tennyson looked at him then back at me. He realized I hadn't told Levi my plan. He nodded then ran off to instruct his group.

Levi waited for me to explain. "Middle name," I said.

"No," he replied.

"Okay," I said, then pretended there was no horse thing.

"Damn it, Grace" he fussed.

"Your choice," I said as I dragged him toward the Shady Grove welcome sign. I touched every tree between here and there, drawing in power.

"I charged this morning at the well," he said.

I had felt him leave the house, but it wasn't unusual for him to go for a morning run. He never went far. After last night, I was in a fog most of the morning, so I did some last-minute prep.

As night drew closer to us, I began to worry. Betty wasn't here, and no one had heard from them.

Another late arrival was Deacon Giles and the Yule Lads.

"It's like having children," he grunted.

We laughed as the 13 trolls bustled around grabbing armor, shields, and clubs from the back of Deacon's truck.

They didn't look formidable, but I was willing to bet they could do some damage. They geared up, then headed to the Food Mart.

Deacon stepped forward offering a twisted horn that looked like it belonged on a goat. Or a Krampus.

"What's this?" I asked.

"You needed a horn to call your hunt. I had two," he said.

"Deacon!" I exclaimed.

"For Dylan," he said.

I gulped, "Won't this make you off balance or something?"

He laughed. "No, but Lamar made me a prosthetic."

"Ah!" I said looking down at the hollowed-out horn. I had intended to substitute Levi's music for the horn in the stories, but I guessed we could go the traditional route. Although, I'd think Krampus horns were pretty rare, and not traditional at all. However, some of the stories that Levi and I had read about the hunt revolved around Yule instead of Samhain. The horn would be our ode to tradition.

"Thank you, Deacon," I said.

He bowed then joined the others.

"They aren't here. Are they still within the ward?" I asked Levi.

"No one has crossed," he said.

"We can't wait any longer," I said. "Time to hide."

Levi leaned over and kissed both of my cheeks. "I've got your back," he said.

"You have no idea," I replied.

"Huh?"

I laughed as I covered my armor with the cloak and pulled the hood over my head.

Levi spoke one word, and I watched him fade to nothing. "Conceal."

I walked to the crest of the hill that once overlooked the trailer park and waited. Levi's senses stretched out to mine. I could feel what he was feeling as he stood behind me.

Voices in the distance like faint whispers on the wind filled the air.

"*I hear my mother. She says she is proud of me,*" he said.

"*The veil has weakened. Our dead speak to us,*" I said listening to the voices of our loved ones. I felt the spirit of our people strengthen. Then a voice called out to me.

"*You have exceeded my expectations, Grace. Please forgive me of my mistakes. Please forgive my daughter,*" Jeremiah's voice said.

"*Gloriana, I am impressed by your resilience. Make him pay, my daughter,*" my Father's voice called out to me.

The one I wanted to hear the most finally came to me.

"*I will love you forever. Now kick some ass, Beautiful Grace.*"

"I will, Dylan. I will for you and our children," I replied to the wind.

A duct-taped Cutlass rolled up behind me. I turned to see Cletus and Tater covered in armor made from plastic milk jugs.

"You two need to get on outta here. You can't fight this fight," I said.

"Well, seein' as how we still live here, we gotta do our part," Cletus said.

"You don't understand," I replied.

"Naw, Grace, you underestimate redneck engineering," Tater said as he dragged a long piece of white PVC pipe out of the trunk of the car.

"What the hell?" Levi said.

"Oh, cool. Look Tater. Levi is invisible," Cletus said.

"Cool," Tater said waving his hand where he thought Levi was. "Well, this here is a Tater gun."

"You named the gun after yourself?" I asked enthralled. These igits weren't fairies but they could certainly captivate.

Tater tilted his head. "Huh. Never thought of it that way before."

Levi snickered.

"No, my Queen, this device shoots Taters," he said proudly. "Big 'ins."

"I can't believe you've lived in the South and never seen a Tater gun, Grace," invisible Levi said.

"It is highly unusual," Cletus added.

"Maybe it's a Texas thing," I said.

"Never been there," Tater said. "We are going to set up behind the sign over there, then surprise them when they show up."

"Guys, I really think this is a bad idea," I said.

"*Let them. I'll keep watch over them,*" Levi said.

"*You won't have time,*" I said.

"You can't make us leave, Grace," Cletus said.

"It's our town too," Tater added.

"This isn't going to end well," I said.

"So be it," Cletus said.

"Alright," I replied.

"Sweet. Cletus, hide the car. We don't want any of these yahoos stealing it," Tater said hoisting the gun up on his shoulder. He winked at me. "You gotta hold it like a bazooka."

"Seems dangerous," I said.

"It is, but I'll look badass doing it," he replied as his partner hid their car behind the vape shop. I could clearly see it from where we were standing. It was like when Aydan played peek-a-boo. He put his hands in front of his face thinking he was hidden when he wasn't.

I could feel Levi shaking his head at them. I could also feel the veil thinning even more. Darkness rolled across the waters of Trailer Swamp turning it to a black mirror with the occasional tuft of green water plants.

"*Shit,*" Levi muttered in my head.

A lone horseman stood in the distance on the swamp. For him and the magical horse he rode, it wasn't water. It was solid. I stepped forward onto the water, and it turned to ice under my feet. The ice spread as far as I could see as well as under the rider. The horse did not falter on the slick surface.

Like me, he wore a black cloak that billowed behind him. I could not see his face, but I hoped it was my Uncle. Killing him here would be vengeance served cold. No return for his treacherous self.

Reaching my power out to my knights once more to see if they were poised and ready to enter the field, I received a message of confidence from each of them. The veil between the worlds weakened. One by one an army of wild fairies filled the forest outside Shady Grove. My knights and I stood at the ready. Nothing was getting in this town. Not on my watch.

CHAPTER THIRTY-ONE

LEVI

"YOU TELL THE BATTLE PART," GRACE SAID.

"Why?" I asked.

"Because guys are better at that kind of stuff," she said.

"I did have a better view of it than you," I said.

"Why did you have a better view?" Winnie asked from across the room. She had been home for a little while, and we had talked about her not answering her phone when we called. She insisted that she was out at the stone circle and didn't have reception. When Grace and I tried to talk to her about Mark, she shut us down saying her relationship with him was private.

"Because your mother kept a secret from me," I said.

Winnie laughed, "Not my mother."

"Right?" I said.

"Enough," Grace protested. "You had your secret, too."

"My middle name was not that big of a deal," I said.

"Actually, it was Uncle Levi," Winnie said.

"Yeah, I suppose it was," I conceded.

"Well, tell the story of the battle. I was too little to remember," Winnie said.

"Even if I tell it, I'm sure Grace will say I'm telling it wrong," I said.

Grace rolled her eyes across the room from us. "I swear not to say anything unless you get something completely wrong," she said.

Her definition of completely wrong was probably not my definition of completely wrong.

"Alright," I said.

Thinking back on that night, I knew it was a pivotal point in my entire life. It changed the course of who I thought I was and who I was going to be. Which was probably why Grace wanted me to tell the story of the battle. It wasn't just a battle between Shady Grove and the Wild Hunt. It was a battle within ourselves to accept the responsibilities that we had taken up. To become the leaders that Shady Grove, the Exiles, and the Otherworld needed.

~

Standing behind Grace, I trembled at the sight of the mounted horseman. His black stallion's eyes glowed blood red, and his sword gleamed in the darkness. I also felt Grace's confidence. She didn't waver.

As the wild fairies formed on each side of the leader, I could make out our competition. The first I recognized were the Red Caps. I'd seen their kind before when Grace fought Lysander right after I moved to Shady Grove. They looked like Greasers from the fifties but had nasty bloody teeth. At least a dozen or more large Ogres towered above the front line of fairies which included two grindylows, trolls, sluagh, ankou, and goblins. They teetered on their toes waiting for the order to charge. In all, there was a force of five hundred.

"Don't lose heart now," Grace said.

"I'm with you," I said. It was all I could say because my heart had dropped to the bottom of my stomach looking at our foe. I was supposed to lead this charge, and I didn't even have a horse. Horse.

"The horse thing?" I asked. Grace giggled but didn't answer.

I felt cold power rush past me to her. She uncovered her head revealing her platinum locks and unicorn crown. She lifted her hands up and shouted, "Stop!"

Time stopped and the rabble froze in place.

A light flurry of snow filled the air as her voice carried on the wind, "I am Gloriana, Daughter of Oberon, heir to the Winter Throne, Queen of the Exiles. This is my home and my people. You will turn back."

The horseman shook off her magic and answered, "You dishonor the dead. The Wild Hunt has come to claim you," he said.

"We will not yield!" she yelled.

"So be it," he growled. From a sheath attached to his back, he pulled a black-bladed sword. His armor and banner were also black with no emblem or markings. He rode along the front-line dispelling Grace's magical hold on his fighters.

In the legends, a black knight wasn't always a bad being. Sometimes it was just a person who wanted to conceal their identity. I assumed that this knight was hiding something as well. I could only guess at who he really was.

Looking more closely at the soldiers, I realized these weren't normal Wild Fairies. Their faces decayed with rot, and their clothes hung from their thinning bodies. They were the dead.

"*Fucking wild fairy zombies,*" I said.

"*Eddie will be pleased,*" Grace replied. I had forgotten the deal we had made with the ghoul. Grace was right. His people were going to love this. If we survived that long.

"Ready?" she asked.

"Yep," I answered holding Excalibur in my hands.

She lifted the horn of Krampus and blew. The rider turned abruptly to face her. Grace blew the horn again. Its haunting call echoed through the town.

The rider laughed, "You have no hunt to call. We have already summoned it." The specters laughed along with him.

A wail floated on the breeze becoming louder and louder. Looking over my shoulder, a woman walked toward us wearing rags. They fluttered in the wind against her green skin and white stringy locks. The cry reverberated as if we were in a small room instead of the center of town.

Betty's lament pierced our ears, and I spoke a spell. "Dampen."

The keen softened, but from her yowling face, I could tell that Betty screamed louder.

"What is the meaning of this?" the rider demanded.

Grace ignored him lifting the horn once again, she blew another haunting call. I stepped out from behind her, dropping my concealment. Excalibur sang in my hands, vibrating a chord produced by my tattoo.

Grace dropped her cloak revealing her armor underneath. Her tattoos flared brightly. When I stepped up next to her, I looked at my own skin explode in blue swirls matching hers.

"You will surrender," she demanded of the rider.

"One man with a sword, even one such as the Great Sword, will not stop the Hunt," he said.

"I'll call your Hunt and raise you another," she smiled.

Two bright portals opened on each side of us. The residents of Shady Grove stepped through following our knights. Each one held their swords at the ready, and Troy leveled his guns at the mob across from us.

Grace's tattoos spread to each person, painting us like warrior Celts.

"It is not a Hunt! You have no leader! No rider!" he scoffed.

"*Levi?*"

"*Yeah, Grace?*"

"*That horse thing,*" she said.

"*Yeah,*" I answered impatiently.

"*It's actually a unicorn thing,*" she answered.

My stance faltered as I looked toward her. She grinned, then shifted to an armored, white unicorn with glistening blue swirls and a crystal horn.

"*Grace,*" I protested.

"*Levi, you will never hear me utter these words again,*" she said, nudging me with her snout.

"*What words?*" I asked.

"*Ride me,*" she said.

There are things that women can say that cause an involuntary reaction in a man. I fucking reacted.

"Holy shit!" I said.

"*And if you pull on this bit in my mouth, I will buck your ass off,*" she added.

"Levi, this isn't time to hesitate," Tennyson scolded. It had been over a year since I'd ridden a horse. And it certainly wasn't a fairy queen, but it was something I knew how to do. Both ways.

Grabbing the horn of the saddle, I swung up on Grace's back. Lifting my sword, I yelled, "For Shady Grove!"

Grace lifted up on her hind legs, and I leaned forward to compensate. When her feet hit the ground, a rush of wind tore across the field towards our opponents.

They braced themselves against the torrent, as we began to advance. Calling on my own skills, I forced music through the strings of my guitar. The thrumming beat matched the pounding of hooves, paws, and feet. Instead of the airy sound of an acoustic guitar, I played the metal tune of classic rock guitar.

More so in this form, I felt Grace's magic supporting us all. Not just me.

As a unicorn, she wasn't just a rare beast. She was *the* rare beast. Looking past her head as we galloped toward the incoming horde, a sparkle caught my eye. Around her horn close to the tip, our engagement ring sat reflecting the blue light around us. I wondered how she planned to keep it there without it falling off during the battle.

"*Pay attention,*" she scolded. She must have felt my thoughts wavering. Raising Excalibur up, we plunged headlong into the fray. The red caps were out front, and the yule lads matched them two at a time.

Lamar's peg was now a bright blade that he used to slice body parts after he brought them down with a large rounded club. Each of the Lads had similar clubs and were using them to bat down the front line as the knights rushed past to the more formidable foes.

I pounded my sword into the troll standing below me. He countered my blows with a long wooden rod. A whizz flew past my ear, and I looked up to see a potato smack a troll in the center of his forehead. His eyes went blank, and his body hit the floor with a thud.

Looking over my shoulder, Cletus and Tater reloaded the gun with a broom.

"*Do not let them pull you off. Our people need to see you still fighting. Still in control,*" Grace instructed.

A large rock slammed into Grace's neck and she kicked sideways.

"*Are you hurt?*" I asked, spinning her around to get eyes on our attacker.

"*No. Focus on the fight. Not me,*" she said.

I spotted a creature who spun a sling around his head. He was misshapen and gangly. His greenish skin festered with boils as yellow snot ran from his pointed nose. He fired again, and Grace dodged the rock.

"*He looks like an orc,*" I said.

"*Close enough. He's Fomorian,*" she said.

I knew the Fomor to be one of the most fiendish villains of Celtic lore.

I batted down a red cap that grabbed my wrist as the Fomor spun his weapon again, but before he unleashed it, a bright sword appeared through his neck. When the dead body dropped, Finley's long white hair stained with droplets of red blood and black ichor billowed around his head. He snarled at me, then turned to battle a new foe.

We continued the fight. With each enemy we dispatched, another seemed to come out of nowhere.

Astor roared with each jab of his sword. His foes piled at his feet.

Troy advanced on a group of trolls with his wolves by his side. He started firing Driggs, and the loud reports echoed above the cacophony of battle. The wolves took down the enemies in pairs, calculating each strike and killing blow. Or bite in their case.

Many of our other friends plowed through the hunt including Chris Purcell, who had a herd of wild boar chasing a winged sluagh.

Rising above the sounds of battle, I heard a chant. Three red cloaked figures stood outside the Magic Vape shop with their hands raised.

"Astor!" I yelled to the ginger knight that was closest to them. He met my eyes then turned toward the trailer. His broad shoulders straightened, and he plowed through the enemy toward the Order of the Red Cloak. His Ella was in that building, and I knew there was no way he would let them in.

"*Let him handle them. We have enough here to worry about. Help is coming,*" she said.

When I faced forward, a large club hit me in the gut. I wheezed as Grace spun me away from the attacking ogre. He stood over us swinging down with his club again. I tried to anticipate Grace's dodge, but we went opposite directions. The club knocked me to the ground, and I scrambled to my feet.

The battle raged around me, but the ogre focused his attack on me. As he pummeled me with the club, I blocked him using Excalibur. He beat down on it, and I pushed my magic down the sword to push back up as he pounded. Several times he got me off balance because I was looking for Grace as I protected myself.

"*Grace!*" I pleaded feeling her close by. The ogre suddenly froze turning to a bluish, ugly block of ice. "Shatter!" I yelled thrusting the sword at him. The strike didn't hit the beast, but my magic rushed out the end of the sword. The ogre exploded into chunks of ice.

Grace stepped through it grabbing me at my neck by the tunic under my armor.

"I said, don't fall off!" she growled. The fear, anger, and frustration in her eyes scared me, but as another attacker lunged toward us, she threw up her hand at it without taking her eyes off me. It, whatever it was, turned into another block of ice.

"Shatter!" I said pointing to the block. It exploded like the ogre.

We repeated the combo several times before we made enough room for her to shift again.

"*Don't fall,*" she demanded.

"*Don't fall,*" I repeated, as I mounted her again.

~

"Nope," she protested. "Rephrase that."

Winnie laughed.

"Grace, it's a common horse term," I said.

"There was no mounting!" she yelled.

Winnie continued to giggle as I teased her further. "What term would you rather me use?"

"Not mount," she said.

"How about astride?" I asked.

"Good one," Winnie said.

"I'm a word god," I said. She died laughing again. Grace fumed, but we ignored her.

"I'm going to meet up with Mark," she said after she calmed down.

"Really?" I said.

"I should apologize," she said. Grace stepped into the other room. I knew what she was doing. Often times Winnie would open up to me. Grace had to be the parent which at Winnie's age made her resent her mother. Being the good mother that she was, she stepped out of the room so that Winnie would talk to someone. Even if that someone had to be me, instead of her.

"What made you decide that?" I asked.

"I see you with Mom. You take her shit all the time, but you still love her," she said.

"Yeah, I do," I said.

"And mom should apologize," she said. I heard Grace growl in my head. I laughed.

"My relationship with your mother is just different. You have to decide what you want with Mark. I suggest though that whatever you decide you be truthful with him," I said.

She thought for a moment then said, "Thank you, Uncle Levi." She kissed me on the cheek then hurried out the door. The Camaro's engine rumbled to life, and Winnie sped away.

"I'm not apologizing," Grace said.

I grinned at her. She folded her arms and stared me down. "That's fine. We both know you've said 'ride me' more than once," I said. Then I dodged a flying coffee cup.

CHAPTER THIRTY-TWO

Levi

Determined to do my duty, I climbed back up on Grace's back. From this vantage point, I could see that Astor couldn't get to the ORCs because of the growing number of wild fairies in the frozen field.

"*Blow the horn again. Summon the ghouls,*" she said.

I grabbed the horn draped around her neck and blew hard. Then again. The wild beings around us paused the fight. Once they started dropping by our blades because of the distraction, they started fighting again.

From every direction, dark shadows raced to the field of battle forming a barrier between the breach and the town. Edward's form solidified, and I heard him call out to the shadows.

"Feast on the wild!" he yelled.

The shadows rushed into the fray. I watched as one opened its mouth to swallow the arm of a troll. The troll squealed like a pig while dripping gore from his stump. The shadow lunged again unhinging his jaw and sucking down the troll whole.

"Yuck," I said, turning back to Astor who had been joined by

Troy and the wolves. They pushed through the crowd. Just before they reached the red witches, three more forms appeared in white robes.

"*Move closer to them,*" Grace said.

We stomped through the fighting horde. I knocked off as many as I could as we galloped through the fight. The white-robed witches chanted to combat the red ones. I could see the faces of the white witches. It was Wendy, Kady, and Riley.

"*Do you see this?*" I asked.

"*Yes,*" Grace said. "*Let the whites work on them.*"

A roar filled the air. Grace spun us around toward the call as a hulking beast stepped out of the mist. It had three heads, and looked like a dragon, but was lean like a dog. A really huge dog.

"What the fuck is that?" I asked.

"It's an Ellen Trechend!" Tennyson said as he ran up next to us. "We could use Luther right about now!"

"*He is coming,*" Grace said.

The hard thump of wind displaced by giant wings filled the air as the flying Ifrit descended upon the battlefield. He landed in the middle with a loud roar which shook the ground. Some of the smaller wild fairies scurried away. The three-headed beast marched toward Luther with purpose. Once within reach, Luther swatted at the Ellen catching along one of its jaws. The lower part of its mouth sagged, barely hanging onto the head. Unfortunately, it still had two perfect heads with jagged teeth. It roared and its hideously bad breath was worse than anything I'd seen on the field. I thought I was going to puke.

It flopped its head back and forth until the lower jaw fell loose, thudding to the ground. It roared with anger charging Luther who took the blow in the chest. The beast held him down clawing at his body and face.

The Ifrit roared back in anger unleashing a flood of fiery lava at the Ellen. It jumped away as the lava splashed off its scales leaving it singed but not damaged.

As they battled, I surveyed the fray. It seemed like we were winning. Just inside the mist, I saw another form. A man on a horse with a straight back. His face was uncovered watching the battle intently. He was beyond the portal, inside the Otherworld.

Gently pulling on the reins, I turned Grace to the man. She lurched forward, racing toward her Uncle. I could barely hang on as her legs churned under her. His eyes widened as I lifted Excalibur. Its shining light drew the attention of the entire battlefield.

I let out a loud yell as we hurdled toward the breach, but as we reached the edge, the portal closed leaving us inside the Vale and Brockton in the Otherworld. The Wild Fairies, realizing that they had been cut off from any escape, began to surrender.

Except for the fight between the Ellen and Luther, the other fights died out. The ghouls consumed the dead and dying. They dragged their corpses below the ground until all the shadows were gone.

"*Levi, get off,*" Grace said.

"*You said don't get off,*" I argued, but before she could respond, I felt her melt beneath me. I landed on my knees straddling her back. The blue lighted tattoos from her power faded from our people.

"Grace! Grace! Talk to me," I panicked. I couldn't feel her or hear her anymore.

Rolling her over, her body was limp and she didn't breathe. Finley ran toward us, but I saw him motioning behind me. I grasped my sword, turning around to block a blow by the black knight. His dark sword slid off mine, as I stood to my feet ready for his advance. Grace's body lay beneath me. I didn't care what I had to do, this evil would have to cut me down to get to her.

Blow by blow, I pushed him off of us in a complete defensive effort. He took several different moves to get to us. I didn't dare look to see if I had help. My only concern was protecting Grace.

"If she dies, all of this goes away," he said through his helmet. "Let me kill her, and you all can live."

"No," I responded with my first offensive strike. He fended it off with a laugh.

"The poor bard taking up a sword that he doesn't deserve hoping he can land the woman he could never have," he taunted me.

I ignored the banter, taking steps toward him. Now he was on the defensive, as I made move after move. He laughed as I put myself into each strike.

A loud groan split through the field, as the Ellen hit the ground in death. Luther had won but was weakened. He sank to his knees, as Betty ran up to brace him.

The death blow distracted us for a moment, but I turned back to the black knight. "You're not welcome here. You were given a chance to leave, and you didn't take it. Now you will end up like him."

Unleashing everything I learned, the knight's eyes turned from humor to concern. I pressed him further and further away from Grace. Finley had reached her and was trying to wake her up. I couldn't look back again or the knight would gain the advantage. I fueled my fight with my anger about Brockton's escape. Pulling power from around me, I pushed winter power into the sword. The knight tried to block my blows, but eventually, he went to a knee, dropping his sword.

"Mercy," he screamed.

I reached above my head with the sword at a high position. "No," I growled.

"Wait!" Tennyson called out. Had it been any other person, I would have ignored them.

"What?" I asked.

"Take off your helm," Tennyson ordered.

The man removed his helm to reveal a handsome, but dark man. His face wasn't scarred, but from the look in his eyes, his soul was.

"Agrevain," Tennyson said. "I should have known you would be helping Mordred."

"You're a traitor, Lancelot. Nothing you can do on the field of battle will make up for you fucking our king's wife," Agrevain said.

"I'm going to kill you," Tennyson replied.

I brought Excalibur down, striking him through the shoulder to his heart. "No, I am," I said, jerking Excalibur out. It hummed with the death as if it loved the kill. I knew the knight's story from

Taliesin's works. He helped destroy the kingdom turning against Lancelot for his affair with Guinevere. Up until that point, Arthur didn't seem to care about the affair even though he clearly knew about it. Eventually, it destroyed the kingdom and the heralded roundtable.

The knight would get no second chance or third chance. He died inside the Vale as Brockton had abandoned the hunt. With the fight over, I noticed that the white witches were joining hands in a prayer to the goddess near where Grace lay on the frozen ground. I didn't see where the red cloaks had gone, but I no longer felt them within the ward.

Running to Grace, I knelt down beside her.

"Has she moved?" I asked.

"No. I don't understand," Finley said. "She isn't wounded."

I searched her armor, removing it piece by piece. We found no wound. However, she lay motionless. The hardest part was that I couldn't feel her. Looking through my sight, the brightened aura from earlier in the day now dimmed with each passing second.

"Grace!" I screamed at her. "You get up!"

"Levi," Tennyson tried to coax me.

"No, don't touch me," I said.

"Levi, the ice is melting," he said.

I looked up as the ice forming the field of battle started to break up. I could hear the cracking and groaning of the swamp trying to push through the ice.

Placing Excalibur in its sheath, I hoisted Grace up, and we ran for the Shady Grove sign. Exile and Wild fairy alike ran for the safety of solid ground as the swamp threatened to take us all. I was exhausted and out of breath once we reached dry ground. Tennyson and the other knights except Astor kept the crowd back as I tried to wake her.

Tabitha ran up to sit next to me. "Let me see her, Levi," she said.

"I can't feel her," I said. "I don't understand what happened."

"It's the magic, Levi. She's tapped. She kept all of us fueled including you. You must have felt it. That cold surging inside of you as you fought. That was Grace's power," she said. "She used it up."

"I'm running on fumes," I said. Looking at the crowd, we all were spent. I ran to the nearest tree which was an oak. Digging deep, I tried talking to it as Grace had shown me.

"*Bard who carries the king's sword,*" it said.

"*Yes, please share your power with me. The Queen has fallen,*" I said. The oak shook above me showering me with leaves. I could feel its sadness. It showed me images of Grace talking to it multiple times. It had a connection with her. Opening up a well of power, it fed me more than I could store. My tattoo glowed in the night as I ran back to Grace.

My guitar played the healing song as I placed my hand over her tattoo.

"*Gracie, come back to me,*" I begged. "*We won. We need you. I fucking need you.*"

Her tattoo flared with power and the curling swirls coursed over her body. Her eyes fluttered focusing in the distance.

"No, just one more moment," she begged.

"One more moment for what?" I asked in a whisper.

"Levi?" she asked. I could finally feel her again.

"I'm here," I said.

"We won?" she asked.

I brushed hair and leaves away from her face, "Yes, we won," I said. "Who were you talking to?"

"Dylan," she said.

CHAPTER THIRTY-THREE

GRACE

As the last of my stored power left my body, I could no longer hold the animal form. I collapsed to the ground. I felt Levi panicking as we careened to the frozen swamp. He managed to redistribute his weight so that he didn't land on me, but after that, I couldn't feel him.

I had seen the black knight approaching. I feared that Levi didn't see him in time.

"Levi!" I screamed out, but my voice echoed like I was in a cavern.

A dim light approached me, then transformed into Lilith. We were inside the tree. I recognized it from my last visit.

"What am I doing here? The battle! I have to get back," I said.

"You used all your power, Grace," she said.

"I died?" I asked. "I can't. I have to go back. My children!"

"Perhaps you should have stayed with them in the vault instead of fighting," she suggested.

"No, I had to be there for us to win," I replied.

"This is true. If you hadn't powered the battle, Shady Grove and all of its inhabitants would have died," she said. "Did you make the right choice?"

"If my children are safe, then yes," I said.

"Don't you care about your bard? The make-shift king?" Lilith asked.

"He has royal blood. He isn't make-shift," I said. "He will be king."

"Will be or is?" she asked.

"It's complicated," I said.

"That's a relationship status, Grace. Is he or is he not the king?" she pressed.

"In my eyes, he is," I said.

"You can stay here or go back. You decide," she said.

"Why do I get a choice and no one else in Shady Grove does?" I asked. "Did Dylan get a choice?"

"You can ask him if you stay," she said.

"What?"

"His spirit is here in the tree of Life. If you decide to stay, you can ask him if he got a choice," she said.

I looked around the tree, reaching out with my senses. I didn't feel his warmth.

"What is this?" I asked.

"What do you think it is?" she asked.

"If I had to guess right now, I'd say it was hell!" I shouted. "Let me go home."

"Is that your choice?" she asked.

"*Come back to me*," Levi's voice echoed through the tree. He sounded broken and desperate. I knew that sound. I'd heard it from my own lips. Felt it with my own heart.

"This doesn't feel right," I said.

"Enough," Astor's voice echoed through the tree.

"Ah, my knight who abandoned me for another," Lilith said.

"Send her back," he said.

"You left here. You no longer get to order me around," she disagreed.

"He is the King of Summer," I said.

"He is not!" Lilith said.

"In my eyes, he is," I said. "Send us both back."

"I came on my own, Grace. Thanks, though," he said with a smile. "I'm not dead. Yet."

"Yet!" Lilith shouted.

"Sometimes she likes being a pain in the ass and someone has to set her straight," Astor said, staring her down.

"Sounds like someone else I know," I said.

He grinned. "True."

"Fine. Go back," she said. "This is the second time I've sent you back. You don't get any more chances, Grace."

"*We need you.*"

"Levi," I said. "I have to go."

"Do you understand, Grace? This is your last chance," Lilith said.

"You do need to acknowledge that much," Astor instructed. "We can talk more about this once we've returned to Shady Grove."

"You have always been a sucker for a pretty girl," Lilith said.

"I know, and my girl is waiting on me," Astor said.

"*I fucking need you.*"

"Damn it!" I said as a figure moved in the shadows. I saw the form of the sandy-haired man that I loved. Dylan. He was here. Lilith grinned as if she had won despite my choice to go back to Shady Grove.

My eyes darkened then fluttered.

"No, just one more moment," I said, looking up into Levi's cobalt eyes.

"One more moment for what?" he asked.

"Levi?" I saw him, but couldn't feel him there. The oath kicked back in suddenly, and his rush of emotions flooded over me. Mostly, he was relieved.

"I'm here," he said.

"We won?" I asked.

"Yes, we won," he smiled. "Who were you talking to?"

"Dylan," I said.

A portal opened behind him, and Astor stepped through. He

knelt down next to Levi taking my hand. I noticed the three white witches standing nearby. I knew the faces of all three of them and was shocked at one in particular. Astor drew my attention back to him.

"Grace, she can make you see things that aren't there," he said.

"I saw him," I said.

"No one was there but her. She has to be watched. Kept in check," he said.

"But she is a goddess," I said.

"She's never been a very good goddess though. Very mischievous," he said.

"Oh," I said. "It wasn't him."

"Probably not," he said.

"I didn't feel his warmth. Just a shadow," I said.

"She was toying with your mind," he said.

"But she's been friendly," I said.

"In your terms, she has multiple personalities. You've seen them. The three in one. Her mind isn't always stable. I imagine the death here tonight drove her a little over the edge," he said.

"Did we lose anyone?" I asked.

"Troy is doing a count," Tennyson said. He was covered in black blood, but Jenny hugged him tightly.

"Your children are asleep in the vault. They are fine," she said.

"The witches," I said.

"The Order of the Red Cloak disappeared, but our very own protectors are still here," Jenny said.

I raised up to look at the three white cloaked witches. The one in the center lowered her hood. Wendy smiled at me.

"I acted alone, but it was the right thing to do," she said.

I cut my eyes to the other two who removed their hoods. Kady Rayburn spoke first.

"I wanted to do something to fight back at Robin. Wendy has been teaching me," she said.

"And you?" I asked looking at the third. An auburn-haired beauty. Finley stood behind her watching me closely.

"Trying to redeem myself," Riley said.

"I'm not sure how you do that approaching Levi in my home in the middle of the night," I replied.

"We should talk about that," she said. "I swear to you it wasn't me. On my life."

There was power in her admission, and therefore, I took it to be truth. If she knew what was going on, I was anxious to find out. I tried pushing myself off the ground, but it was harder than I thought it would be. My body was still drained, but regaining power by the moment. I felt it rushing to me as if I were in the Otherworld.

"Easy," Levi said, supporting my back. My eyes focused on the townspeople. They were cut and bruised but living. I felt each one of them. Cletus and Tater waved at me.

"Help me up," I said.

Levi put his arm around my waist, steadying me as I stood. Astor stood in front making sure I didn't fall forward. The crowd cheered as I stood. They began to hug each other and shake hands. Troy walked up to us.

"I'm happy to report, everyone is accounted for," he said.

"It's a miracle," I said.

I heard a groan from behind me. Turning to look, Betty braced Luther who seemed to have taken the brunt of the battle with the Ellen.

"Luther," I said.

"I am alright, my Queen. Just a little out of practice," he said.

"Practice! You're too damn old to be running around fighting dragons," Betty scolded.

He grinned. "I love you, woman." He kissed her hard, and she batted him away.

"Stop it. You, crazy old man," she said. "Not in front of the youngins."

I leaned on Levi as I watched the people of Shady Grove celebrate the victory.

"Levi?"

"Yeah?"

"I want to go home," I said.

"I'll bring the kids to you," Jenny said.

"Thank you," I replied.

"Alright, Dublin," I said.

"Home," he said. I felt the power he held swirl around us. After the fight, I was drained, but he wasn't. I wondered if he had a supernatural battery.

We appeared in the darkness in front of the house. The night was cool and quiet. We stood there in the stillness for a moment. I could feel his heart beating. The relief that I was alive.

"What's wrong?" he asked.

"Remember when the witches cursed me?" I said.

"Yeah," he said cautiously.

"And I died."

"I remember," he said.

"She sent me back then too," I said.

He moved in front of me, looking into my eyes. "What do you mean?"

"Lilith said she sent me back one other time. She said this was my last chance," I said.

He groaned leaning into me. "Then no more dying."

I wrapped my arms around his waist. "No more dying."

CHAPTER THIRTY-FOUR

IT TOOK SEVERAL DAYS TO RECOVER MY STRENGTH FROM THE BATTLE at Trailer Swamp. A small vacation from the Queen duties allowed me to spend time with my children. Winnie had calmed down a little since the battle. She had heard stories around town about how her mother and Uncle Levi lead the charge against a bunch of bad guys.

The carnage of the fight was swallowed up by the swamp. The parts that the ghouls didn't consume. Eddie and his group seemed content to let Betty stay with us here, as long as I contacted them the next time we decided to prepare a feast.

Aydan now said, "Momma" on a regular basis. Along with something that sounded like "Weevi," which was completely adorable.

My experience with Lilith and the tree was explained further by Astor. It was why he was so initially timid to allow me to go to the tree when I was in Summer. Lilith had a split personality, and some days she was a benevolent goddess. Others, she was batshit crazy.

Astor sat across from me as Ella rubbed a concoction on his back. He had a large circular bruise from the fight.

"Where did that come from?" I asked.

He grunted, and Ella giggled. Levi looked up from his laptop with a twinkle in his eye. I had a pretty good idea where it came from, but I wanted to tease the ginger knight.

"Potato," he said.

Levi couldn't hold back, and he died laughing. Aydan sat beside him eating his lunch. Winnie laid on the floor with Rufus, coloring. I sat back and enjoyed the laughter of my family. I hadn't stopped missing Dylan. I didn't think I ever would stop, but after the battle, I valued the things I had much more than I had before it. The pain was easier to bear. I fueled it into my plans to kill Brockton.

"*You're thinking too deeply over there,*" Levi said from across the room.

"*Just appreciating what I have,*" I said.

"*Two beautiful children,*" he said.

"*And a set of loyal knights,*" I said.

"*And Astor,*" Levi added. I giggled. Ella looked back and forth between us, shaking her head. She had gotten used to picking up on our mental conversations.

"*And a very brave poet king,*" I said.

Levi knew I wasn't teasing him. I meant it. He was the official mayor of Shady Grove now. The Protector of the Vale. I still wore the ring he gave me. Most people knew we weren't engaged, but it was still a symbol of my dedication and support.

The intense moments we had leading up to the battle had more to do with the extreme situation of Dylan's death and the pressing need to do something about the Otherworld than the constant frustration that both of us felt because of our mutual attraction. We defeated the Wild Hunt as a team. I found that humbling myself, allowing him to lead was the right thing to do in that situation.

We had discussed it multiple times since then. At times I was so determined to do things myself that I had lost sight of the things that made Shady Grove and my life different. I had a family. People to depend on, and people that depended upon me. Lilith and my father both believed that I had it within myself to do this alone. However, I had decided that alone was not how I wanted to do it. I wanted these people in my life. I wanted them in my heart. Even if it was a risk.

Losing Dylan was painful, but in the way a heart hurts when it's lost someone. Not that I would have never wished it to happen in the first place. My children held a very big part of that heart now, but so did Levi.

I'd been a rebel my entire life, fighting against the expectations. Right now, the expectations were that he and I would end up together. I couldn't deny it was a possibility. He didn't press the issue, and I didn't pursue it. If the time was right, we would know. For now, I think we were both content and still deeply connected.

"He's getting so big," Levi said as he hoisted Aydan out of his chair.

I laughed as Aydan's fat belly poked out beneath his shirt.

"Look at that belly," Ella said.

Levi patted his belly and said, "Aydan, look at your belly!"

"I think he ate too much," I said.

"I agree. He's thicker than a bowl of oatmeal," Levi said, lowering him to the ground. He held his hands as my chubby baby waddled over to me.

"Momma!" he said reaching up to me. I lifted him up on the couch where he sat in my lap. Levi sat down next to me, and I leaned on his shoulder.

"You good?" he asked.

"So good," I said.

He wrapped one arm around my shoulder and poked Aydan's belly. Aydan laughed like a doughboy. I reached up and poked him too. His little laugh filled the room. Winnie grinned at us playing with her fat, happy brother. I was so blessed.

"Lordy mercy, Aydan, you're fuller than a tick!" I exclaimed.

CHARACTER LIST

Grace Ann Bryant- Exiled fairy queen hiding in Shady Grove, Alabama. Daughter of Oberon. Also known as Gloriana, to her Father and the fairies of the Otherworld. She was called Hannah while traveling with the gypsy fairies before coming to North America. Owns a dachshund named Rufus. Loves orange soda and Crown. Nickname: Glory

Dylan Riggs- Sheriff of Loudon County, Alabama. Fiancé to Grace Ann Bryant. The last living Thunderbird and the only living Phoenix. Also known as Serafino Taranis and Keme Rowtag. Nickname: Darlin'

Levi Rearden- Changeling from Texas brought to live with Grace by Jeremiah Freyman. Given Bard powers by Oberon. Looks good in a towel. Nickname: Dublin

Wynonna Riggs- formerly known as Wynonna Jones, but adopted by Grace and Dylan. Human daughter of Bethany Jones who dies in Tinsel in a Tangle. Given the power of the Phoenix by her father. Nickname: Winnie

Aydan Thaddeus Riggs- son of Dylan Riggs and Grace Ann Bryant. Heir to Thunderbird inheritance.

Nestor Gwinn- Grace's maternal grandfather. Kelpie. Owner of Hot Tin Roof Bar in Shady Grove. Maker of magical coffee.

Troy Maynard- Police chief in Shady Grove. Wolf shifter. Married to Amanda Capps and father to his adopted son, Mark Capps (Maynard) who is Winnie's best friend.

Betty Stallworth- wife to Luther Harris. Waitress at the diner. Flirts with everyone. Fairy.

Luther Harris- head cook at the diner. Ifrit.

Tabitha Mistborne- fairy physician. Daughter of Rhiannon. Dating Remington Blake.

Mable Sanders- former spy for Oberon. Fairy Witch. Girlfriend of Nestor Gwinn.

Sergio Krykos- Grace's Uncle who has taken over the Otherworld. In his first life, he was known as Mordred, half-brother to King Arthur. Goes by the name Brockton.

Oberon- King of the Winter Otherworld. Grace's father. In his first life, he was known as King Arthur.

Rhiannon- Queen of the Summer Otherworld. Half-sister to Oberon. In her first life she was known as Morgana, a fairy witch.

Remington Blake- Grace's ex-boyfriend. Dating Tabitha Mistborne. From N'awlins. Sweet talker. One of the Native American Star-folk.

Astor- The ginger knight that Grace brought back from the

Summer realm. Formerly betrothed to Grace. Former First Knight of the Tree of Life. In his first life, he was Percival, Knight of the Round Table.

Matthew Rayburn- Druid. Spiritual leader of Shady Grove. Leads services in a Baptist Church which is a portal into the Summer Realm. Enthralled by Robin Rayburn.

Kadence Rayburn- Daughter of Matthew. Ex-girlfriend of Levi. Enthralled by Malcom Taggert. Becomes a fairy. Dating Caleb Joiner.

Malcolm Taggart- Incubus that once tried to seduce Grace. Enthralls Kady.

Caleb Joiner- Lives with Malcom and Kady, but frees Kady from Malcolm.

Riley McKenzie- Daughter of Rhiannon and Jeremiah Freyman. Levi's ex-girlfriend. Stole the songbook. Fled the Summer Realm with Grace.

Stephanie Davis- Daughter of Rhiannon. Dylan's ex-girlfriend. Sergio Krykos' ex-girlfriend. Mother to Devin Blankenship. Missing in the Winter Otherworld.

Joey Blankenship- Tryst with Grace. Enthralled by Stephanie. Father to Devin Blankenship. Turned into a faun by Rhiannon. Escapes the Summer Realm with Grace and his son.

Eugene Jenkins- Mayor of Shady Grove. Former Knight of the Round Table, Ewain. Wife died in childbirth. Father to Ella Jenkins. Partner to Charles "Chaz" Leopold.

Eleanor "Ella" Jenkins- Changeling daughter of Mayor Jenkins. Catches Astor's eye. Teacher at the fairy school.

Charles "Chaz" Leopold- Also known as "The Lion." Hairdresser. Second Queen in Shady Grove.

Finley- Grace's "twin" brother. Married to Nelly. Wears armor portraying the symbol of Grace's royalty.

Jenny Greenteeth- A grindylow living in Shady Grove. In her first life, she was known as Guinevere, wife of Arthur, lover of Lancelot. Cursed to her current form.

Tennyson Schuyler- Mob boss. In his first life, he was known as Lancelot, Knight of the Round Table. Oberon calls him Lachlan.

Cletus and Tater Sawyer- Last human residents of Shady Grove. Comical, but full of heart.

Yule Lads- A group of Christmas Trolls who moved into town. Lamar is the most frequently mentioned with his various peg legs. Others include: Phil, Cory, Willie, Chad, Keith, Kevin, Phillip, Ryan, Bo, Richard, and Taylor.

Michean Artair- Solomonar. Owner of Magic Vape. Produces magical liquids for all occasions.

Brittany Arizona- Shady Grove's tattoo artist.

Bramble and Briar- Brownies who live in Grace's house, but are attached to Winnie. Hired by Caiaphas to watch over Grace. Now in servitude to Grace.

Caiaphas- Leader of the now defunct Sanhedrin. Former Knight of the Round Table.

Fordele and Wendy- King and Queen of the Wandering Gypsy Fairies. Fordele was Grace's lover ages ago.

Josey- Grace's former neighbor in the trailer park. Perpetually pregnant. Goddess of the Tree of Life. Also known as Lillith.

Jeremiah Freyman- Deceased. Former member of the Sanhedrin that brought Grace, Dylan, Levi, and most of the other fairies to Shady Grove. Worked for Oberon. Father of Riley. Former Knight of the Round Table. Known as Tristan.

Deacon Giles- Farmer in Shady Grove. Krampus.

Connelly Reyes- First Knight of the Fountain of Youth. Former Knight of the Round Table known as the Grail Knight, Galahad. Best friends with Astor.

Chris Purcell- Winged-werehog. Known as a dealer of information. Settled in Shady Grove with his domesticated wife, Henrietta.

Lissette Delphin- Creole Priestess. Tricked Levi into summoning the demon, Shanaroth.

Rowan Flanagan- Partner of Tennyson Schuyler. Died in Summer Realm. Mother of Robin Rayburn. In her first life, she was known as Elaine. Mother of Galahad.

OTHER MINOR CHARACTERS

Kyffin Merrik- Former partner in Sergio Krykos law firm. Missing.

Demetris Lysander- Grace's former lawyer. Deceased. Aswang.

Phillip Chastain- Judge at Grace's hearing in BYH. Helps with legal matters. Liaison to Human Politicians.

Misaki- Oni disguised as a Kitsune.

Elizabeth Shanteel and Colby Martin- human children murdered in BYH by Demetris Lysander.

Rev. Ezekiel Stanton- Pastor of Shady Grove Church of God. Evacuated when the humans left Shady Grove.

Sylvestor Handley- Michael Handley's father. Blacksmith.

Diego Santiago- Bear shapeshifter. Executed by Grace.

Juanita Santiago- Bear shapeshifter. Widow. Mother of two. Oversees a farm with Deacon Giles help.

Niles Babineau- Developer from New Orleans that helped Remington Blake build more housing in Shady Grove. Returned to New Orleans.

Jessica- Summer fairy working at the sheriff's office.

Stone and Bronx- Tennyson Schuyler's bodyguards.

Eogan- Treekin in Summer Realm.

Marshall- Captain of the Centaurs in Summer Realm.

Nimue- Lady of the Lake. Keeper of Excalibur. Controls the Water Element Stone.

Brad and Tonya- Brad owns the BBQ joint in Shady Grove. Tonya works there as a waitress.

Katherine Frist- Fairy woman living in Shady Grove known for her many dead husbands.

Ellessa- Grace's Siren mother. Whereabouts unknown.

Melissa Marx- Levi fangirl.

Taleisin- Bard for Arthur and many other Kings and Rulers. Wrote the songbook given to Levi.

Thistle- Purple haired pixie with a love envelope.

Sandy- Matthew Rayburn's Nurse

ACKNOWLEDGMENTS

To my grandparents who used more of these phrases than I do now. I remember them saying these things and came to appreciate the uniqueness that is the Southern dialect.

To my BETA group and the group of great folks at Magic and Mason Jars. You guys are why I am motivated to keep putting out books. I have my own fulfillment in them, but your enthusiasm takes my love to a whole new level

To Jeff, my hero, and Maleia, my princess. I love you both immensely.

From early in life Kimbra Swain was indoctrinated in the ways of geekdom. Raised on Star Wars, Tolkien, Superheroes and Voltron, she found herself immersed in a world of imagination. She started writing in high school, and completed her English degree from the University of Alabama in 2003.

Her writing is influenced by a gamut of authors including Jane Austen, J.R.R. Tolkien, L.M. Montgomery, Timothy Zahn, Kathy Reichs, Kevin Hearne and Jim Butcher.

Born and raised in Alabama, Kimbra still lives there with her husband and 5-year-old daughter. When she isn't reading or writing, she plays PC games, makes jewelry and builds cars.

Join my reader group for all the latest updates on releases, fabulous giveaways, and launch parties.

Follow Kimbra on Facebook, Twitter, Instagram, Pinterest, and GoodReads.
www.kimbraswain.com

CPSIA information can be obtained
at www.ICGtesting.com
Printed in the USA
LVHW041031040520
654954LV00002B/488